HOW TO SURVIVE A Classic Crime Novel

HOW TO SURVIVE A Classic Crime Novel

Kate Jackson

First published 2023 by
The British Library
96 Euston Road
London NW1 2DB

ISBN 978 0 7123 5438 7 (paperback)
ISBN 978 0 7123 6801 8 (e-book)

Cataloguing in Publication Data
A catalogue record for this book is available
from the British Library

Illustrations by Joanna Lisowiec
Designed and typeset by Briony Hartley, Goldust Design
Cover by Rawshock Design
Printed in England by CPI Group (UK), Croydon CR0 4YY

CONTENTS

After what seemed like an endless night, your Bakelite alarm clock rings loud enough to wake the dead. It is time to put our cards on the table. You are in a classic crime novel. In London, one of the deadliest of cities. Bleary eyed, you stretch and climb out of bed, ready to face another day in a world where behind every door and face, murder potentially lurks. Trust nothing. Trust no one. The reader is warned. Murder is easy, they say, in the classic crime universe. Every day a murder is announced, or at least it feels that way. It's not quite murder every Monday, but nor is sudden death all that uncommon.

To survive this dangerous world, you need to proceed with caution. Prevention is essential. If you have already imbibed the poison, then it is too late to find the cure, the antidote to venom. Murder must be nipped in the bud. Everyone's under suspicion, from the man in the brown suit and the laughing policeman to the local busybody and even the woman in the wardrobe. (Yes, people do pop up in some rather surprising places in classic crime novels!) You may be wondering: how do I stay safe? The answer is: read this book! It is packed with crucial tips to avoid a premature death. Don't go anywhere without it.

But there is no time to waste! Get washed! Get dressed!

Downstairs, you finish tidying up from last night's entertainment. Ashtrays are emptied, the fireplace is cleaned, and the dirty crockery is taken to the kitchen to wash up. Only just in time do you remember to leave a note out for the milkman and put the rubbish out for collection. That nearly put the cat among the pigeons. You have earned your breakfast. But before you chomp down on a slice of toast and pour yourself a cup of tea, it is time to begin your first lesson in survival …

LESSON 1
Home Sweet Homicide

Before you are ready to dodge the traps waiting for you outdoors, you need to avoid the ones that might be hiding inside your own house. After all, most accidents happen at home and an accident – or rather, what appears to be an accident – is the perfect camouflage for a would-be murderer. Don't be the fool who says: '*This is your own home, isn't it? Nothing to be afraid of in your own home.*'[1] So, let's start in the kitchen …

Cooking Up a Crime

While you are unlikely to meet your demise within this room in an Agatha Christie mystery, the kitchen is often used by prospective killers for preparing their deadly weapons. A poison can be sprinkled into a half-prepared meal in a matter of seconds. But this plan can be thwarted in several ways:

1 Never leave your cooking unattended, and avoid being distracted by others. Better still, just don't allow anyone else in the kitchen in the first place!
Source: Christie's *4.50 from Paddington*[2]

2 Always stay to supervise if someone else insists on making the food.
Source: Christie's *Sad Cypress* and Anthony Rolls's *Family Matters*

3 Don't become complacent about using pre-prepared food and ingredients. Even your everyday kitchen oil can be substituted for a deadly poison.
Source: Douglas Clark's *The Gimmel Flask*

4 Remember to check your milk bottle tops too! While a mischievous blue tit might be responsible for the hole in the top, there is also the possibility that it was put there by human hands to inject a poisonous substance inside. Don't take the risk and pour it away.
Source: Sidney Carroll's 'A Note for the Milkman'

5 If someone gathers fresh food for you, ensure the items collected are safe to eat. Buying a book on foraging is a smart move, meaning you can check any comestibles you are presented with. You will soon know your foxglove leaf from your sage!
Source: Christie's 'The Herb of Death'

Bear in mind that murderers can use fungi, such as mushrooms, as scapegoats. Unlike Adriana Ford in Patricia Wentworth's *The Silent Pool*, you might not have a fly, the domestic equivalent of a miner's canary, to alert you to the lethal nature of your lunch, and hiring human food tasters is rather expensive. And before we leave the kitchen, here are a few other foods we suggest you leave off the menu …

Starter

You might be keen to try an almond-based starter, but this nut could prevent you from tasting any cyanide in your snack.

Source: John Rowland's *Murder in the Museum*

Main course

Not only are shish kebabs tricky to eat, but the skewers they come with can also be deadly. Can you identify if a skewer has been made from oleander branches?

Source: Hildegarde Dolson's *Please Omit Funeral*

Dessert

Stay clear of the hundreds and thousands on the trifle, especially if no one else is eating them!

Source: Christie's 'The Tuesday Night Club'

HERE ARE A FEW MORE HANDY TIPS ...

Our researchers have gleaned further advice from pertinent case studies.

1: Richard Hull's *Keep It Quiet*

Do not store poisonous substances in the kitchen inside innocuous-looking containers. Others may only see the vanilla essence label and not realise they are putting perchloride of mercury into the soufflé instead. Even if you are not the one who dies, having a corpse on your hands is rather inconvenient, as it leaves you vulnerable to blackmail.

2: Jonathan Stagge's *Death, My Darling Daughters*

Silver polish must always be removed correctly from silverware. Cyanide poisoning is not the ideal accompaniment to afternoon tea. To be on the safe side, use plastic crockery. It may be less fancy, but it doesn't require polishing.

3: Christie's *The Moving Finger*

Keep sharp implements such as knives and skewers under lock and key – and make sure you have the only key!

Sleeping Murder

Statistically, in a Christie novel, the bedroom is where you are most likely to be bumped off, so be especially on your guard there.

Now for a tricky question: Should you lock your bedroom door before you go to sleep?

a. Yes, obviously! I want to keep the killer out of my room!
b. No, I need to be able to leave in a hurry.

This is a question which caused much debate within the Classic Crime Survival Research Unit (CCSRU), but ultimately it was concluded that there does not need to be a strict rule, as a murderer's plans are not necessarily foiled by such a ploy. Neither Harriet Steele in Rupert Penny's *Sealed Room Murder*, nor Lady Ironmonger from Patricia Moyes's *Black Widower* was saved by this tactic. One helpful tip is to lock your bedroom door when it is not in use, as this protects your belongings from being tampered with. As always: learn from the mistakes of others!

Case study: *Thou Shell of Death*
Author: Nicholas Blake
Date: 1936
Victim: Knott-Sloman
What the victim did: Cracked open a nut which had been poisoned, with his back teeth.
What the victim should have done: Used a

nutcracker. The contaminated nut would have been easily discernible and therefore avoided.

Case study: *Murder Is Easy*
Author: Agatha Christie
Date: 1939
Victim: Amy Gibbs
What the victim did: Reached out in the night for her cough medicine and instead swigged toxic hat paint.
What the victim should have done: Turned on her light. Checked she had the correct bottle and that the fluid inside was her medicine. Smelling the bottle or pouring out a little of the contents would have aided this task.

Case study: *Death by Request*
Author: Romilly and Katherine John
Date: 1933
Victim: Lord Malvern
What the victim did: Owned and used a gas heater in his bedroom.
What the victim should have done: Removed the heater the moment he moved into the property and used an alternative form of heating. Gas-operated appliances must be avoided at all costs.

An additional benefit of locking your bedroom door is that no one can add extra stress to your day by depositing a corpse in there! It may seem unlikely, but Augusto de Angelis records such a case happening in the 1940s in a Milan fashion house in *The Mystery of the Three Orchids*.

BEDROOMS WITH A REPUTATION FOR KILLING PEOPLE

Cases of bedrooms that seemingly kill their occupants have been recorded for a while, from L. T. Meade and Robert Eustace's 'The Mystery of the Circular Chamber', to John Dickson Carr's *The Case of the Constant Suicides* and *The Red Widow Murders*. Even today, 'killer' bedrooms feature in TV shows such as *Jonathan Creek*.

The first way to avoid this danger is simply not to enter the room. Take a sleeping bag and slumber elsewhere. Even the garden shed would be a better place! If you own the house, you might wish to take a leaf out of the Westmacott family's book, as in Martin Porlock's *Mystery at Friar's Pardon*, where the younger family members quickly decide to sell, once they see their forebears bite the dust – each time in the bedroom. Conversely, do not follow Bertram Deaves's example and buy such a house, dismissing its well-documented reputation.

If staying in the room is unavoidable, make sure you stay with more than one person. A group is best. Killer rooms tend to be less deadly with larger numbers.

Try to touch as little as possible and don't use the bed. Keep the windows closed and covered to prevent attack from the outside.

Lastly, don't stick your head out of the window! Ignore all provocation to do so. Don't play into the killer's hands like Mary Gregor did in Anthony Wynne's *Murder of a Lady*. Moreover, if you ignore this advice you will also be making your death even harder for the sleuths to solve, by dying in a seemingly impossible manner. There's no need to be that inconsiderate!

KEY SKILL

Gift of Death

Receiving a present can be an exciting surprise. But beware! While there might not be any trojans concealed inside your gift, presents of chocolate are very hazardous and must be approached with extreme caution.

Never eat chocolate in the following circumstances:

- The chocolate was unexpected, even if the label states that the parcel has been sent by a relative. Lady Stranleigh got caught out this way in Christie's 'The Voice in the Dark', as did Marcia Tait in Carter Dickson's *The White Priory Murders*.

- The chocolate was a freebie from someone who didn't want it. Yet another lady fell foul of a deadly chocolate bounty this way in Anthony Berkeley's *The Poisoned Chocolates Case*. The title says it all!

Death in the Bathroom

In most cases the bathroom is a safe place. However, Anthony M. Rud's *The Rose Bath Riddle* is an exception: someone tampers with the shower, so liquid nitrogen is sprayed through the shower head. The odds of this happening to you are slim, unless you are living with a disgruntled chemist who is a dab hand at DIY and plumbing. In that situation stick to using dry shampoo instead.

If this does not apply to you, the bathroom can be a useful location. Unlike most rooms in the house, it has a lock on the door – and if Susannah Shane's *Lady in a Million* is anything to go by, getting locked in your bathroom by others for a prank can provide a handy alibi. Furthermore, if you concur with Fredric Brown's idea that 'a bathroom without a bookshelf is as incomplete as would be one without a toilet',[3] at least you will have something to do while waiting to be released.

The police, however, may be less pleased with you, as your value as a witness dwindles considerably if you happen to be bathing while someone else is getting killed. As shown in Patricia Wentworth's *Who Pays the Piper?*, the police take a dim view of the claim that the noise of the hot water pipes can prevent someone from hearing a murder. They may even suspect you did the deed yourself! If you find yourself in such a situation, a haughty and indignant manner may help. You could even borrow this line from Anthony Gilbert's *Tenant for the Tomb*: 'People having baths don't expect to be asked to act as witnesses.'[4] Please don't throw away your toiletries and buy a job lot of nose pegs, or you might become the first person to be bumped off for excessive body odour!

In contrast to bedrooms, research suggests that locking the bathroom door and windows when in use not only spares you a lot of embarrassment, but can also prevent your untimely demise. The victims in both Gladys Mitchell's *Speedy Death* and Erle Stanley Gardner's *The Case of the Velvet Claws* can attest to that. Keep your personal grooming routine short to increase your survival rating. Now could be a good time to consider growing a beard. Gilbert Wynter in Cecil Waye's *Murder at Monk's Barn* would certainly have wished he'd given it some more thought. Oh, and don't forget that an unclosed window is an open invitation to a local murderer on the lookout for a place to dump a body. Keep your window locked if you don't want to be like Thipps in Dorothy L. Sayers's *Whose Body?* and find something worse than a giant spider in your bath in the morning!

AGATHA CHRISTIE'S BATHROOM CHECKLIST

Keep the following items locked away securely to prevent tampering:

❑ **Nasal spray**
Source: *The Mirror Crack'd from Side to Side*

❑ **Eye drops**
Source: *Crooked House*

❑ **Shaving cream**
Source: 'The Cretan Bull'

This last example shows that tampering is not always done to achieve immediate death. Other desired effects include causing the victim to suffer hallucinations and to act oddly. This is useful if the killer wants their victim perceived as being of unsound mind.

❑ **Compile a medicine inventory**
Source: *A Caribbean Mystery*

This may seem like an unusual suggestion, but an accurate record of any medications you take can hinder a killer who wishes to obscure the true cause of their victim's death.

On a final note, caution is advised when renovating your bathroom. Be careful what type of bathtub you choose. Safety is more important than what is trending. One recommendation we received from Colonel Sherran in Anthony Gilbert's *Death Knocks Three Times* is to avoid baths with lids. They are definitely a pain in the neck! And if you are anything like the couple in Margot Bennett's 'No Baths for the Browns', then you may find more than you bargained for when you begin to demolish your old bathroom.

Who's Been Sitting in My Chair?

Whether you call it the lounge, the living room or the sitting room, you still need to know how to stay safe when you are puzzling over Torquemada's latest crossword in the armchair or elegantly reposing on the chaise longue while enjoying a new Paul Temple mystery on the wireless.

When it comes to room temperature, views are divided. Some prefer it cool, while some like it hot. Yet in the classic crime universe, those who choose the extra jumper over lighting the fire may have a survival advantage. Open fires are dangerous in many ways. You might be thinking of the deadliness of the flame, but what about the poker or tongs? Hanging by your fireside are these perfect instruments for murder when your back is turned. In Christie's *Taken at the Flood*, victim identity is even obscured through such a weapon. However, even if you decide to keep your fire tools locked away, there are still other possible roles for your fireplace within a murder plot. Hiding a body is one of a killer's greatest challenges, and over the years chimneys have been a popular space to conceal a corpse. An early recorded case can be found in E. M. Channon's *The Chimney Murder*.

Alternatively, you might have opted to use only central heating. But does that leave you danger free? Unfortunately, the answer might be no if the killer decides to disable your electric lighting to hinder visibility. An open fire in that situation would have spoilt their plans. But before you reopen the fireplace, a simpler solution would be to keep an eye on your fuse box, and Christie's Miss Marple would recommend being vigilant about replacing any frayed electrical wires.[5]

However, it is not just your lighting which can be tampered with for murderous purposes ...

Death on the Air: Could You Spot if Your Radio Had Been Made to Kill? Sign up for Agatha Christie and Ngaio Marsh's

RADIO SAFETY COURSE,

which helps participants get to grips with the inner workings of a radio and how to check if they have been altered.[6] With their handy tips it will be disappointed faces all round when your wannabe killers see you foil all their attempts.*

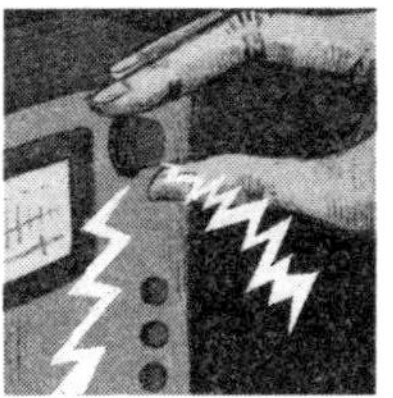

Course coming soon: E. C. R. Lorac and John Bude's Killer Telephones – Or, Why You Should Always Let the Maid Answer the Telephone.[7]

* Christie and Marsh take no responsibility for anyone who uses their safety materials to kill someone rather than protect themselves.

KEY SKILL

Maid for Murder

While it is rarely the butler who did it, you still need to know how to keep him on side. Blackmail or damaging witness statements to the police are the problems you are more likely to face, whether you just have a daily help or have the full complement of staff below stairs.

Here are two actions to avoid:

1. Never reveal anything incriminating if you might be seen or overheard. Phrases such as 'I could kill you' or 'I wish you were dead' should never be uttered.

If a murder investigation occurs, it is possible that your servants will share all your secrets with the police. Don't be like one woman who wrote in to us, crying: 'Up until that moment I had given no thought to our servants or the importance of what they would have to say.'[8] If your secret is of a murderous nature, you are open to blackmail. You might cope if your bank balance is healthy but otherwise you are inconveniently left to plan another murder.

2. Never overlook new members of staff.

Are they really who they say they are? Does that

jawline remind you of someone you know? Take a closer look. Christie would certainly recommend it![9]

One issue that has caused much furore is whether domestic staff should be given a TV. Do you risk your housekeeper leaving you, unless a TV is installed in the kitchen?[10] Or do you risk the potential for violent TV dramas to influence how your housekeeper expresses her dissatisfaction towards you?[11] Which will you choose? The possibility of a gory death or the bleak prospect of having to wash your own dishes and do your own hoovering? Tough choice.

A Study in Scarlet

For a long time, the corpse in the study has been considered a cliché. Amateur detective Colonel Gethryn, as early as 1924, complained of it when faced with such a death: 'No originality! … It's all exactly the same. Ever read detective stories …? They're always killed in their studies. Always! Ever notice that?'[12] Yet how true is this? The CCSRU decided to investigate the matter. Evidence gathered from John Dickson Carr and Anthony Berkeley showed a tendency for studies to feature in locked-room murder cases.[13] However, researchers using the longer case studies recorded by Christie were surprised to discover only four murders in the study, the same number as happened in the hallway!

Nevertheless, whether the study is an original place to die or not, it is important to be aware of the hazards that lurk there. After all, you have no way of predicting if your would-be murderer yearns to kill in a creative fashion, or what detective literature they have used for research. Use the map below to gauge how many dangers your study might be concealing.

Door

Do not enter your study at night.

Source: Marion Harvey's *The Mystery of the Hidden Room*

French windows

When building your study avoid having a garden entrance to the room, as this widens the field of suspects if you get murdered. If your study already possesses such an entrance, try to keep facing it when using the room, so no one can sneak up on you.

Sources: Christie's *The Murder at the Vicarage* and *A Blunt Instrument* by Georgette Heyer

Desk drawer with key in lock

Dangerous objects such as guns and personal comestible items should be kept under lock and key. Although, really, if you are keeping loaded weaponry in your study then you are just asking for trouble!

Sources: Marie Belloc Lowndes's *Motive* and *Excellent Intentions* by Richard Hull

Radiators and gas heaters

Gas heaters should be avoided. In the classic crime universe studies can easily be made airtight and you would not be the first person to bite the dust through gas poisoning, yet

have your murder believed to be a suicide.
Source: Carter Dickson's *He Wouldn't Kill Patience*

KEY SKILL

A Will in the Way

Wills and their contents have indirectly caused innumerable murders. Perhaps a poor relation is itching to get their inheritance, or maybe another legatee fears they will be cut out of the family fortune. If you are looking to make a new will there is one golden rule to remember: **DO NOT TELL ANYONE YOU ARE CHANGING YOUR WILL UNTIL YOU HAVE DONE SO!** Heed this warning from Mavis Doriel Hay's *The Santa Klaus Murder*! Countless men and women could have saved their lives if they had followed this simple rule. Little sympathy is held for those who ignore it, even less so if a forthcoming will change is being deployed as an ultimatum. In such a scenario you have signed your own death warrant. If your offspring are about to start a job you disapprove of, or – worse – marry someone you loathe, you are just going to have to find a different way of dealing with it. Finally, a last piece of advice on wills from Christie: beware of invisible ink![14]

The Body in the Library

Who hasn't held a long-cherished dream of having a personal library at home, with the perfect comfy spaces for reading and endless rows of bookcases with sliding ladders? But is it safe for you to have such a room? Are you better off going to a public library instead? Take this quiz to find out ...

1. Are you a wealthy person?
A: Yes
B: No

2. Do family members hold grudges against you?
A: Yes
B: No

3. Do you frequently lock yourself, alone, inside your library?
A: Yes
B: No

4. Do you enjoy playing party games inside your library?
A: Yes
B: No

5. Does your library have hidden passage-ways or doors?
A: Yes
B: No

Results

Mostly As …

The bad news is that having your own home library could take years off your life, and not in the way a moisturiser might do. There are strong feelings about this from recorders of crime such as Dorothy L. Sayers. She once wrote: 'I am confirmed in the opinion that no millionaire should ever enter a library.'[15] Anthony Berkeley also proves the point that extensive precautions to prevent killers from getting inside your library are futile:

> *The hunted look that for the last few days had been sitting so incongruously upon the rugged features of Mr Algernon Dinwiddie, the millionaire Bradford mill-owner, was even more pronounced than usual as he locked himself into his empty library, fastened the shutters carefully, stuffed his handkerchief into the keyhole and double-locked the ventilator.*
>
> *'Safe here, thank God,' he muttered with a sigh of relief.*
>
> *The next moment he fell to the ground with a loud report.*[16]

Party games are a lot of fun, but Christie in *Hallowe'en Party* warns readers to avoid any water-based activities. Not only will your carpet be ruined, but there is always the possibility someone may take the opportunity to drown someone. That person might not be you, but do you want to take the chance?

If you are adamant you are keeping your library then having the room checked for hidden doors and passageways is of the utmost importance. These features may give a room character or history, but they also provide a handy way for would-be murderers to secrete themselves in the room without you knowing about it. Both Christie's *Spider's Web* and Michael Innes's *Appleby and Honeybath* reveal the deadly consequences of not following this advice. Another thing to consider is that by possessing a sizeable home library you might be required to host amateur sleuths wanting to share the solution to a local crime to the set of suspects. Sleuths, especially amateur ones, are rather fond of having an audience in a library. Perhaps they have better acoustics ...

Overall, if you are in this group, going to a public library might be safer. Reports of murders occurring there are fewer than those at home. However, it would still pay to keep an eye on other library users around you and maintain an antisocial distance from them. After all, in 1931 Charles J. Dutton recorded a case of a librarian who was strangled while within calling distance of several others.[17]

Mostly Bs ...

Good news! You are safe to have a library of your very own. Now you just need the money to make one. If only you knew someone who got mostly As in this quiz ...

Common or Garden Crime

Having considered the dangers your house might hold, you wouldn't be blamed for thinking it is safer to stay in the garden. Yet you would be wrong! From the old can of weedkiller which no one can find, to beehives laced with poison, your garden poses many threats. It's time to see how much attention you have been paying. Can you spot the five dangers in this garden?

So how did you do? Check with the answers below.

1. The swimming pool

In the classic crime universe, as testified by Victor L. Whitechurch and Patricia Wentworth, swimming pools are corpse magnets![18] Organise a garden party and you can guarantee by the end your pool will have a dead body. Stroll down to breakfast and you can bet the missing person will be found there. Think of the cleaning expenses! Pool safety inspectors Frances and Richard Lockridge and Dana Chambers also point out that emptying the pool does not decrease your chances of a corpse.[19] Nor does using someone else's swimming pool without their permission! Winifred and Orson Otis in the Lockridges' case file, *A Client is Cancelled*, certainly got a grim surprise when they chose to have a skinny dip in a friend's pool one night.

2. The well

Like the pool, wells are another way you could meet a watery end. However, what makes wells a sneakier peril is that they can hide a body much more effectively. This efficacy is increased if the well is old, disused or little known. For further reading on this hazard try:

- Francis Vivian's *The Singing Masons*
- Moray Dalton's *The Strange Case of Harriet Hall*
- Brian Flynn's *The Creeping Jenny*

To reduce the potential danger of wells and swimming pools, it is strongly advised you fill them in, post haste!

3. The summer house

If you are planning a clandestine meeting in the summer house, make sure you don't leave any telltale signs of your presence behind. Christie shows us, in her famous mystery *The Murder of Roger Ackroyd*, the awkward conversations that ensue if you don't follow this rule. If murder has occurred, a torn item of clothing or a missing piece of jewellery can all put you one step closer to being arrested – a danger which is also recorded in Annie Haynes's *The Crystal Beads Murder*.

4. The heavy statue

A classical sculpture or a stone memorial to a family ancestor may seem like the finishing touch to your garden, but Father Brown warns that they may seem less idyllic if you are squished underneath one.[20] Despite their weight, you would be surprised how easily they can be manipulated to fall just as you are passing by them. It goes without saying that if you are invited to anyone's garden party, stay clear of the statues at all costs.

5. The wasps' nest

Wasps, in the world of classic crime, pose more of a threat than a painful sting, as they provide opportunities for killers to conceal their felonies. A wasp's nest provides a would-be murderer with a legitimate excuse for buying poison, as is the case in Christie's 'Wasps' Nest', but the criminal does not necessarily need to be the purchaser to be tempted into using it for murderous purposes.[21] Poisons aside, a wasp's nest can also become an unexpected place for a murderer to cache their weapon. Keep your eyes peeled for telltale stings to the hands or face in particular – although we do recommend leaving it to the police to execute the search of the nest for such an item. After all, wasps are not the most amenable to having their home raided for murder weapons, as John Davies can painfully attest.[22] Bees, overall, tend to be less aggressive, but that hasn't stopped them from being trained by human hands to turn deadly. For more detailed case notes on this danger see Anthony Wynne's 'The Cyprian Bees' and H. F. Heard's *A Taste for Honey*.

KEY SKILL

Don't Feed the Animals

It is said that canines are man's best friend, but in the classic crime universe they have an uncanny ability to nose their way into a crime – be it the cause of one, the mechanics of the crime, or the solving of it. Here is some advice to help you and your pooch avoid the more negative ways a dog can get involved in crime:

- ☛ Ensure your garden is effectively dog-proofed, so they cannot escape into your neighbour's garden and be a nuisance. Not everyone will take the destruction of their prized begonias lightly and you could be in for a nasty surprise.
  Source: Henrietta Clandon's ***Good by Stealth***

- ☛ Always tidy away your dog's toys after they have finished playing with them. An ill-placed ball at the top of the stairs is all too easy a set-up for a murder which is meant to look like an accident.
  Source: Christie's ***Dumb Witness***

- ☛ When on a dog walk, be prepared to encounter new and unexpected information. Walking

> your dog in a cemetery appears to increase the likelihood of this event occurring. However, be warned, this information is not always positive. Sometimes it will aid you in solving a case, if you are an amateur sleuth, but it can also thrust into your life some alarming personal information. You may get more than you bargained for!
> Sources: Christie's ***Postern of Fate*** and Margaret Millar's ***A Stranger in My Grave***

Dogs are not the only risky pet to have. Horse riders need to be mindful of attempts to murder them by spooking their horse. Solo hacks are to be avoided, as are early morning ones, especially in a rural area, since there are likely to be fewer witnesses around. These all conspire to make you an easier target. This advice applies to confident riders too, as while you might get lucky, like Susan Kerr in Philip MacDonald's *The Choice*, you could end up sharing the same fate as Violet Feverel in Stuart Palmer's *The Puzzle of the Red Stallion*.

The criminally minded also need to watch their step with animals. Earl Derr Biggers and Anne Austin would recommend avoiding committing a crime or talking about it afterwards in front of a parrot.[23] There are some things you won't want repeated! Not every crime involves a murder; some are just concerned with theft. But beware of using an animal as a way of concealing your stolen goods. This is a plan which can spectacularly backfire, as anyone who has read their Sherlock Holmes will know.[24]

Despite the rush, you are on time for heading out to work. The London Particular, a hazard in its own right, is out in full force. Make sure you pull your coat and scarf around you tightly. The fog is dense but the street outside your home is still bustling with life. Commuters and delivery drivers are jostling for pavement space. It's no wonder you trip over a trunk near your house that is waiting to be picked up. Thank goodness you don't end up in the middle of the road. Otherwise, your life and this book would be cut short. Not that those around you would have minded all that much. Just another death of a fellow traveller. Pick yourself up. Wipe the sticky grime off your fingers. Dust off that brush with death. At least in the fog no one could see you embarrass yourself. But it is not just the deadly climate you have to be mindful of. You still face the question of which mode of transport to take to work. Which method poses the least peril? Will a train ride become the end of the track for you? If you go by foot, will you become another 'incident' at a corner? On joining a crowded bus, how do you know that death isn't coming too?

LESSON 2
Murder En Route

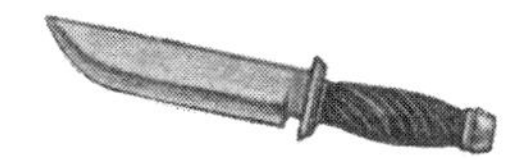

The years between the world wars, especially the 1930s, saw an increase in travel, whether by plane, train or automobile, and the classic crime universe reflected these changes. Just look at the cases Agatha Christie published from this decade. Seventy-five per cent of the crimes she records involving murders set on a mode of transport occurred during the 1930s. So how can you avoid adding to these statistics? Read on to find out …

Coffin Underground

London has had an underground railway since the 1860s, and the primary danger it poses to you is the camouflage it provides would-be murderers. At peak times such areas are congested with commuters. In these crowds you can laugh at any police officer getting a reliable statement from passers-by to help identify your killer. While you might be tempted to wear a suit covered in spikes to discourage any murderous shoves, the CCSRU suggests the following less cumbersome strategies …

Stand clear of the platform edge when waiting for the train to arrive.
Source: Christie's *The Man in the Brown Suit*

Hold on to the supportive railing tightly when using the escalators or stairs to and from the tube station.
Source: Henry Wade's 'The Real Thing'[1]

During off-peak and quieter times, exit the station as quickly as possible. No dawdling!
Source: Mavis Doriel Hay's *Murder Underground*

Be cautious when shaking hands with a fellow passenger.*
Source: Baroness Orczy's 'The Mysterious Death on the Underground Railway'[2]

Do not board an empty carriage, especially when a serial killer is on the loose.
Source: John Oxenham's 'A Mystery of the Underground'[3]

* This might seem rude, but for your own safety we recommend never shaking hands with somebody wearing an elaborate ring or a coat with long sleeves. Both fashion trends could be concealing a poisoned spike. This advice is especially pertinent if there is a chance of the fellow passenger being an enemy of yours in disguise. If you are desperate to avoid being antisocial, we suggest wearing metal gauntlets.

Beware of the Trains

This section is not a repetition of the advice you have just read, as due to train journeys usually being longer, there are further hazards you need to be aware of. Before you even begin your trip, our correspondent from Mexico, Todd Downing, warns travellers to avoid using train lines which involve remote stretches of track if railroad strikes or sabotage are likely. It inevitably adds to your travelling time and as Hugh Rennert in Downing's report *Vultures in the Sky* can attest to, these travelling conditions make it more stressful to find a murderer.

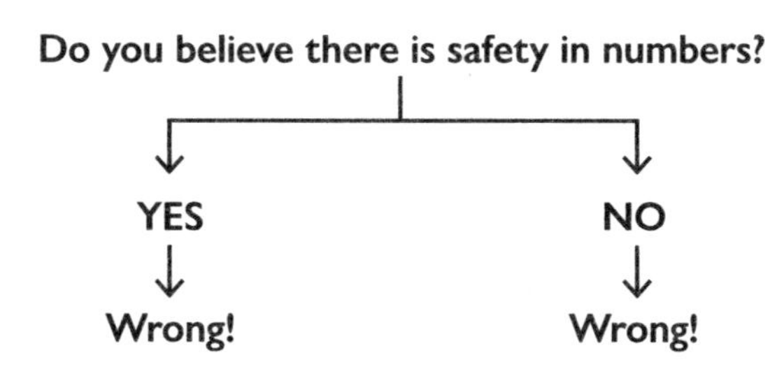

Unfortunately, murder loves company as well as going it alone. You can be strangled in a sleeping berth shared with four other people,[4] as well as shot in a carriage only you occupy. By yourself, you must keep an eye on all entry points into your compartment, including the skylight. Sir Wilfred Saxonby in Miles Burton's *Death in the Tunnel* learnt this lesson the hard way! Building on lesson one, you also need to guard all food and drink, since your ability to ward off attackers is significantly impaired if you doze off. Sleeping medication is naturally to be avoided.

Samuel Ratchett certainly made himself an easier victim in Christie's *Murder on the Orient Express* by ignoring this advice.

There are many hints for keeping safe in multiple-occupancy train compartments. However, you might find not all the tips are relevant. To find the advice most pertinent to you, answer the question below, choosing the options which fit you best:

Which traveller are you most like?

Traveller A: Carriage Drama Queen

While you might perceive yourself as someone who has high energy, a strong need for emotional expression and a youthful zest for living life to the full, it must be said that sometimes you put other people's backs up, especially when your social dramas take over. The danger for you is that your intensity risks giving others the impression that you are crazy or hysterical, particularly if you are trying to convince them of the existence of a passenger no one else admits was on the train. Moreover, if you have alienated yourself from others through inconsiderate behaviour, you might find it hard to call upon them for help to back you up.

Further reading: Ethel Lina White's *The Wheel Spins*

Traveller B: Carriage Daredevil

You will know you fit this category if people often say you 'leap before you think'. The main danger for you is your curiosity. Your desire to immediately investigate a suspicious circumstance or object, especially if there is

the possibility of a body, is likely to be strong. But if you want to avoid a painful bump on the head, we advise you to look around first to check for any potential attackers.
Further reading: Alice Tilton's *Cold Steal*

Traveller C: Carriage Patsy

To the selfishly and even possibly criminally minded, you are easy pickings. Your own honesty and trusting nature mean you are unreliable when it comes to assessing the characters of others. Sometimes you're right, sometimes you're wrong. The danger is to be found during those latter occasions, which can stem from seemingly minor problems, such as a passenger stealing your coat when you leave the carriage temporarily. This might seem like a small irritation, but these things can spiral out of control and plunge you into murder!
Further reading: Conyth Little's *The Black Coat*

Traveller D: Carriage Sleepy Head

While your power to sleep practically anywhere (even on the proverbial washing line) normally means you are envied, this ability could be your downfall. When sleeping you are vulnerable to all manner of manipulation, including waking up in the wrong bed and finding your original luggage has been swapped, as well as your clothes. Even worse, your 'new identity' could leave you as the lead suspect in a murder case!
Further reading: Mary Roberts Rinehart's *The Man in the Lower Ten*

Traveller E: Carriage Chatterbox

You are likely to be this person if you believe you have lots of interesting stories to tell about your own experiences, yet find your close companions are surprisingly quiet individuals who tend to utter the occasional 'You don't say?' Well, without you a social occasion would be akin to a graveyard. But be careful which anecdotes you share. Tell the wrong story and you might give someone a motive to murder you.

Further reading: M. M. Kaye's *Death in Berlin*

YOU'VE REACHED YOUR DESTINATION!

Before you pat yourself on the back for surviving the train journey, bear in mind the following advice, culled from two case studies:

1. J. Jefferson Farjeon's *Thirteen Guests*

Be careful how you alight from the train, as any injuries incurred will impede any amateur sleuthing you are planning on doing.

2. Raymond Postgate's *Somebody at the Door*

Do not become complacent once you have left the station. There is still the walk home to face. Always keep an eye out for anyone following closely behind you.

KEY SKILL

There Came Both Mist and Snow

Snow and fog can quickly derail your travel arrangements, but poor decision-making during bad weather can lead to some deadly situations.

Decision 1: You ignore the forecast predicting heavy snowfall and decide to go on that long car journey.

Consequences: Inevitably your vehicle will get stuck in the snow, and you will be forced to seek shelter. Yet your options for emergency accommodation may be severely limited.

Option A: Isolated country house

Due to the snow, once you have made it to the house, you won't be leaving any time soon. But what will you have let yourself in for? Commercial traveller Dilys Hughes faced such a situation when her car got stuck in a snow drift in rural Yorkshire.[5] While initially she was happy to be out of the cold, she soon found herself up to her neck in crooks, murder, a shootout and, even worse, curry and spaghetti for dinner!

Option B: Isolated country inn
While at an inn you will find more people in a similar pickle to your own, there are downsides.[6] Are there people there who might wish you ill? Will you be under the same roof as your enemy? If you don't know them, you can't verify who they say they are, and you have no idea of their game plan. Have they got their eyes on your valuables?

Decision 2: You are too impatient to wait for your train to be dug out of the snow and decide to go on foot to the nearest house to ask for shelter.

Consequences: You have chosen a far more dangerous option than staying inside the carriage. The risk of getting lost in the snow is high, especially if you do not know the area. However, if you do manage to locate a home, you have no idea what you are jumping head first into. Will there be a crime scene, or will you get caught in the middle of a crime being acted out? Moreover, if others have followed your lead, you are again stuck in a confined space with strangers whose intentions may be less than harmonious.[7]

Decision 3: You decide to travel in foggy conditions. This can be a harder weather problem to avoid, but there are several pitfalls to watch out for.

Pitfall 1: Losing your travel companion. This in turn will make it hard for you to prove your alibi if a local murder occurs.
Source: Christianna Brand's *Fog of Doubt*
Pitfall 2: Becoming the target of a kidnapper. Fog makes you much more susceptible to being a victim of this crime and, as Nurse Deane points out, letting your rescuers know where you are being held is harder than you might think:

> *Again she remembered the book heroines who drop hairpins in a steady trail from the fatal stairway to the murderer's lair, or the men in the Chestertonian romance who had spilled soup and broken windows to leave evidence of their passing. Only had one ever really believed those stories? They didn't happen in real life. Detectives looked for something more subtle than a trail of hairpins, and anyways two plain brown combs and a Kirby grip wouldn't make much of a show.*[8]

Source: Anthony Gilbert's *Don't Open the Door*

Pitfall 3: Your observational skills will be impaired, which can have several consequences. Firstly, you could fall off a cliff edge when answering a call of nature. It won't just be your dignity which is in a bad way. Alternatively, you might fail to spot from your train window whether a murder has taken place

outside, and if so where. Finally, a would-be killer may use the fog to their own advantage and push you into endorsing a false alibi.
Sources: Charlotte Armstrong's 'The Second Commandment',[9] Josephine Bell's *Bones in the Barrow* and E. C. R. Lorac's *Two-Way Murder.*

Death Goes by Bus

Whether you are travelling far or just locally, you need to be aware of the specific dangers buses hold for you. It is a form of public transport where you are likely to be in close proximity to others, which increases your chances of being murdered at close range. To hinder attacks involving pointed instruments, such as knitting needles,[10] we recommend you wear thick clothing, irrespective of what your barometer tells you. If the bus is running a local service, listen out for how frequently it misfires. If it misfires a lot, you would be better off finding a different bus, as the noise provides the perfect camouflage for anyone wanting to shoot you.[11] Given the choice of where to sit on a bus, we all have different ideas of where is best, but the CCSRU strongly advises you to avoid the top deck, particularly if it is an open-topped one and if you are alone. This last factor may seem counter-intuitive, but in fact it increases your chances of being the target of an impossible crime, as the victim of Brian Flynn's *Murder En*

Route can tell you. Finally, be wary of how much personal information you share. The journey might be long, and you might be bored, but you can jeopardise your plans if you reveal them to the wrong person or if someone overhears them.[12] Take a trusty detective novel to fill the time instead!

KEY SKILL

Who's Calling?

There's nothing worse than being dragged out of your comfortable seat by the phone ringing, only to find it is a wrong number or someone playing a prank. Or is there? In the classic crime universe there are many, often deadly, reasons someone may send you a hoax message.

Reason no. 1: Criminals may use a hoax phone call to make you leave your property, so they can commit a murder within your home.

Danger rating: 3/10 (This poses the least personal threat, but it does entail you having police rummaging through your drawers and a big mess to clean up afterwards.)

For further advice, see: Christie's *The Murder at the Vicarage*, John Rhode's *The Telephone Call*[13] and Philip Macdonald's *X v. Rex*.[14]

Reason no. 2: Your killer may lure you from the safety of your home, using a hoax phone call or note asking for your urgent assistance. In this message they will lead you to the location where they plan to murder you. Therefore, when possible, try to verify requests for help and take someone else with you. You are more at risk of this type of hoax call if you are part of a profession which helps others, such as a clergyman, doctor or detective. Detectives, particularly amateur ones, should be wary of hoax calls hinting at the promise of crucial new evidence. Both John Bude and E. C. R. Lorac chronicle the deadly consequences of not following this advice, in *The Sussex Downs Murder* and *Bats in the Belfry*, respectively. If you are emotionally involved with someone, the hoax message may try to play upon your heart strings by suggesting they are in danger. You should be especially on your guard if you are sent to an isolated area such as a wood or a derelict building.

☠ **Danger rating: 10/10** (This is the biggest danger, since your limited information will make it harder to thwart your killer's attack.)

For further advice, see: Christie's *The Man in the Brown Suit*, Lynn Brock's *Q. E. D.* and E. C. R. Lorac's *Fire in the Thatch.*

Reason no. 3: A murderer may use a hoax message to draw you to the location of another person's murder, so you become the police's prime suspect.

Danger rating: 6/10 (The danger level is dependent on the circumstances. Was there anyone else at the crime scene? Do you have a motive for killing the victim? Is there any forensic evidence which could incriminate you?)

For further advice, see: John Bude's *The Sussex Downs Murder* and *Death in White Pyjamas*.

Walk with Care

Given how lethal public transport can be, you might be thinking that walking would be the safer option, and if you follow the rules below, it probably will be.

It does not matter which area of the classic crime universe you are in,[15] one of the biggest dangers of walking to work, along a busy pavement, is the chance of being pushed into oncoming traffic. It is bound to be considered an unfortunate accident. So stay away from the road edge, particularly if you find yourself in a Patricia Wentworth novel.[16]

Avoid solitary nocturnal walks. Christianna Brand's *Green for Danger* especially advocates this rule if you are a witness in a murder case. Do you know something that could expose the killer's identity? Or perhaps you are an obstacle to the murderer's end goal. Either way, stay indoors once it gets dark.

Carefully assess the situation before wading in to prevent a murder in progress. In some cases, a well-timed action may save a life, as is recorded in Phyllis Bentley's 'A Question of Timing',[17] but in other circumstances, if you are in an unfamiliar secluded area and it is foggy, it might be less wise to get involved. Do not follow Caroline Emmett's example and indecisively hang around too long, as the murderer may clock your presence and add you to their hit list.[18]

Calling All Cars

Although we have already covered the dangers of driving in snow, the CCSRU has pulled together some other useful advice from its case study archives ...

1. John Rhode's *Dr Priestley Investigates*

The rule to not drink and drive is one you are likely to be familiar with: an instruction given to reduce the risk of knocking someone over. Trying to conceal such an incident is never to be recommended, especially if Albert Campion is in the vicinity.[19] However, Rhode records a less well-known peril of drink-driving: someone dumping a corpse in your car. Depending on your level of intoxication, you might not even notice the new addition; if you do, you face a difficult job convincing the police that you are not responsible for the murder.

2. Richard Hull's *The Murder of My Aunt*

Car maintenance is an important task to carry out. It lowers your chances of a breakdown, which no one wants, especially on a long journey. However, checking your car over for defects is also an essential way of ensuring no one has sabotaged the car in your absence. It may just mean the loss of some petrol, but it could be something worse.

3, 4 and 5. Annie Haynes's *The Blue Diamond*, Dorothy Cameron Disney's *Death in the Back Seat* and Joel Townsley Roger's *The Red Right Hand*

These case studies have been grouped together as they both offer the same advice: do not pick up hitchhikers. Nevertheless, their reasons for this advice differ. Haynes chronicles a case involving a hitchhiker who could jeopardise your wedding, while Disney records how a hitchhiker can land you in hot water with the police, when, upon arriving at your destination, you realise they have died in the backseat, without you noticing. How can you prove your innocence? Finally, Roger warns of the potential danger of the hitchhiker trying to murder another passenger.

6. Headon Hill's *The Comlyn Alibi*

Do you want £1,000? Well, all you must do is race someone else's car in a speed-restricted area, and if you are stopped by the police, use the name of the car's owner. Sounds like easy money, right? But you might want to think twice before you pick up your driving gloves, as your actions could be securing the alibi for a murderer.

7. Jack Trevor Story's *Mix Me a Person*

Story discourages stealing a car to impress your date with, especially if it belongs to a criminal. You may find yourself arrested for something worse than theft. Try a bunch of flowers or some chocolates instead.

KEY SKILL

Poison in the Pen

No one enjoys receiving a poison pen letter, even if the contents bear no grains of truth. But how often is that the case? Don't be fooled by the surface-level harmony, is what E. C. R. Lorac would tell you. In *Murder in the Mill Race*, she notes: 'Villages, as you may know, are not really more virtuous than towns. They only look more virtuous, and are more successful in coating the past with lime wash, as they do their cottages.'[20] The important thing is not to lose your temper and turn on each other. If you want to see how *not* to follow this advice, read June Wright's *Reservation for Murder*. A key way to restrict a poison pen letter writer is to lock your typewriter away when you are out, and be careful who you let borrow it. This strategy reduces the chances of you being incriminated in other crimes, as well as the sending of the letters. Philip Banter and Dr Amos Truppen both wish they had followed this advice.[21] If you are tempted to try writing poison pen letters, remember they are not the best way to deal with grievances against your neighbours. However much your neighbour has hurt you, the law will be unlikely to take your side. Edna Alice discovered this the hard way.[22]

After much consideration, you opt to walk to work. Well, you don't fancy making the headlines – 'Last Seen Hitchhiking ...' (so undignified!) – and nor do you wish to brave the Underground. Avoiding being near the roadside and giving your fellow pedestrians a wide berth, you progress on foot. You try to convince yourself that walking is not such a bad idea after all. Only last night, you had been thinking that you needed to get some more exercise. Your arms, however, do not agree, given the extra weight they are carrying. Doing errands for a friend can be so tiresome, and for a time you muse over the demands made of you by others. The milk of human kindness is in short supply first thing in the morning. Nevertheless, just before you worry you might drop dead from exhaustion, and before you are tempted to jettison your load into the Thames, you find yourself outside the St Dunstan's charity shop. Despite the shop being packed with rush-hour customers hoping to pick up a quick bargain before dashing to work, you are able to complete your mission and leave your donations by the till. A volunteer will soon notice their presence. Your good deed done, and your arms considerably lightened, you too join the deadly race of employees hurrying to be on time for work.

LESSON 3
Murder Is My Business

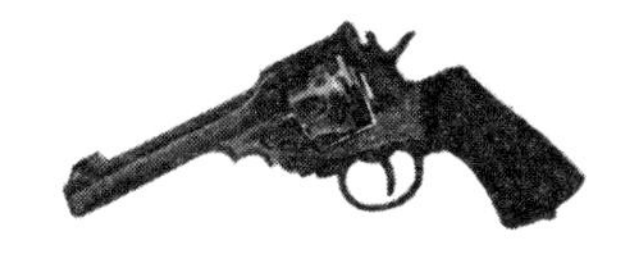

Having survived the commute to work does not mean you can drop your guard yet. Murder can happen just as easily at your workplace as in a country house. Many jobs require you to spend lots of time in the company of others, and this close proximity can quickly breed irritation, resentment and jealousy. The lure of promotion or a pay rise has caused more than one person to stab a colleague in the back, and not always metaphorically … Read on to discover how you can avoid such pitfalls.

It has long been recognised, in the classic crime universe, that business people occupy a high-risk category when it comes to identifying the most popular careers for victims. Yet the features that make a business career so hazardous can be shared with other forms of employment. Check below to see whether your job meets the high-risk criteria.

- ❑ Have you relocated to another country due to being unpopular at home?

- ❑ Have you made enemies through your workplace actions, such as making deals or contracts?

- ❑ Do you use unscrupulous tactics at work?

- ❑ Is your spouse younger than you?

- ❑ Do you rarely accept input from colleagues when making important decisions?

- ❑ Do you use the wealth from your career to control the actions of those close to you?[1]

The more of these criteria you meet, the more likely you are to be killed. However, those in lower-paying jobs should not become complacent. Even a humble box-office cashier can be in peril when they stand in the way of criminals who are intent on embroiling their cinema in a gambling con.[2]

Moment of Decision

Perhaps you are trying to decide upon your first career, or maybe you are looking to switch to a new one. Finding employment can be difficult. What sort of job should you be looking for? How should you go about contacting potential new employers?

SEVEN TOP TIPS FOR FINDING YOUR NEXT GREAT JOB

1 Have a clear idea of what you want to do. If you don't know then it is possible that potential employers might not either.

This is especially important if you place an advertisement looking for work, as it is harder to correct any wrong assumptions. Here is an example of what you shouldn't write: 'Two young adventurers for hire. Willing to do anything, go anywhere. Pay must be good … No reasonable offers refused.' Such wording leaves you open to accusations of criminality, as well as the risk of becoming a victim yourself.[3]

2 Don't base your career choices upon brief romantic encounters.

What are you willing to do to follow a man you had lunch with once? Fake references to gain a job to be closer to them? Relocate to the country they are working in? Victoria Jones was willing, and she had to learn the hard way that adventuring as a career is far from glamorous, and above all that it is important to get to know someone before committing to them.[4]

3 Heed warnings given to you concerning new places of employment.
While it is possible that a rival is trying to clear the field and nab the new job for themselves, there is a chance the warning is kindly meant. To decide which it is, try to identify what reasons this warning was given for and verify if possible.[5]

4 Be wary of being employed at places which have built-in ways of disposing of bodies.
Examples include breweries (vats), pottery works (kilns) and anthropological museums (boilers).[6]

5 Check your place over for job-specific equipment which could be turned into murder weapons.
You might think this problem is more common in construction-type jobs, but even a seemingly innocent office can be full of potential weapons. Examples include buttinskies used in telephone exchanges and bodkins in government and legal offices.[7] You might look silly, but wearing a hard hat to work could save your life.

6 Be cautious of job offers involving easy money for minimal effort.

Learn from the mistakes of David Marks.[8] He accepted a job where all he had to do was drive a mysterious woman to a remote house in the dark. He was paid well for his time, but on the third occasion, when the passenger never returned, he entered the house (always a no-no) and found a dead body – with himself in the frame for murder. Other job offers to be wary of include ones that insist on you changing your personal appearance (for a non-acting job),[9] and ones that pay you lots of money to copy out the *Encyclopaedia Britannica*, especially if you are asked to work away from home.[10]

7 When meeting a prospective employer whom you found through a job advert, always tell your friend about the interview details.

This may seem over the top, but more than one hopeful job applicant has gone missing after attending such an appointment, and a key to their return has been the fact someone knew they were going to the job interview in the first place. Extra caution should be taken if a serial killer is on the loose and is using job adverts to lure in their victims. Don't be like Jenny Morgan, who said when challenged as to why she was going to answer such an advert, despite matching the killer's victims' profile: 'But those things don't happen to oneself.'[11] Oh yes they do!

KEY SKILL

The Great Insurance Murders

Insurance, in theory, is designed to benefit you, providing financial compensation when things go wrong. But sometimes insurance can be used in less honest ways, and these plans often go awry and lead to murder. Never get involved in tontine insurance schemes. Such schemes can be family affairs, one of which George Bellairs records in *Dead March for Penelope Blow*, but J. J. Connington shows us that they can also be found in sporting contexts such as horse-racing syndicates.[12] The problem with tontine schemes is that the temptation to take all the money invariably proves too much, and soon the body count begins to rise. We advise steering clear of life insurance scams for similar reasons, especially if you are required to be the person who must fake their own death. Inconveniences aside, you might find out that your confederates would prefer you to be dead for real. Finally, committing arson is never the answer to solving financial problems at work. The police are unlikely to be fooled and there is much that can go wrong in setting up the fire. To explore the pitfalls of insurance schemes more fully see Ethel Lina White's

The First Time that He Died and George Bellairs's *Surfeit of Suspects.*

The Office Secret

The office can be a minefield at the best of times, what with trying to avoid being the centre of the water-cooler gossip and doing your utmost not to get into your supervisor's bad books. However, there are further precautions you can take to minimise your chances of being murdered at the office.

❑ Don't work alone after hours. An office by yourself can be useful, but it leaves you vulnerable to attack. Schedule all meetings during normal working hours.
Sources: Nicholas Blake's *End of Chapter* and James Corbett's *Death by Appointment*

❑ Always lock your office when you leave. This makes it harder for anyone to set up a booby trap in your office.
Source: Henrietta Hamilton's *Answer in the Negative*

❑ To avoid nasty surprises, make sure storage boxes are not big enough to hide a body in.
Source: Michael Gilbert's *Smallbone Deceased*

❑ Watch your drink at the Christmas party, as toasts are a perfect opportunity for would-be poisoners. This is especially important if you happen to be an unlikeable boss.
Source: Rex Stout's 'Christmas Party'

❑ Avoid having affairs at the office.
Source: Nicholas Blake's *Minute for Murder*

A Scientific Terror

Similar to construction jobs, a scientist's workplace potentially houses hundreds of lethal items which could be used to bring about someone's demise. Therefore a key safety tip is to securely lock away all dangerous substances and formulas. This is not just to preserve your own life, but also the lives of others. Be wary of anyone from outside your job who comes to visit, even a friend. They say they have come for a chat – but are they really after a poison? Even a stolen truth serum can lead to fatal results ...[13] How at risk you are may also depend on the nature of your work. Any job dealing in important scientific formulas automatically increases your risk, as Sir Claud Amory and Michael Harsch learnt to their cost.[14]

The Case of the Good Employer

Those in positions of power and greater responsibility tend to be at greater risk of being murdered. However, our researchers have compiled some useful tips for achieving the optimum employer–employee relationship ...

1 and 2. Eilís Dillon's *Death in the Quadrangle* and Agatha Christie's 'The Nemean Lion'

You won't get the best out of your employees if you bully or manipulate them to toe the line. Employee reprisals will vary from threatening letters to more serious actions such as kidnapping your beloved pooch for ransom or even leaving your pet without its owner. It is hard to say which job sectors are more prone to these problems, although Eilís Dillon does question the murderous capabilities of academics:

> *The surprising thing was that he had been left so long alive. Possibly what had saved … [Bradley] was the fact that professors are not usually practical people. Even if they worked out a dozen methods of murdering Bradley, unless they could hand on the actual task to a research student, nothing would ever be done.*[15]

3 and 4. Margery Allingham's *The Fashion in Shrouds* and Kathleen Moore Knight's *Exit a Star*

Make sure you can trust your employees not to leak your designs or plans. In the classic crime universe, aside from secret formulas, drawings for new clothing lines are also hot property and tend to go walkabout if you don't keep a close eye on them.

5. Dorothy L. Sayers's *Murder Must Advertise*

Take care of your staff by ensuring that your workplace adheres to health and safety standards, as any hazardous parts of the building are liable to be incorporated into a killer's plans. Replacing rickety metal spiral staircases is a definite start in the right direction.

6. Anne Nash's *Said with Flowers*

The last thing you want at Christmastime is employees off sick, as you can certainly feel the pressure to fulfil all your orders. However, we urge you to always get references before hiring new employees. Anne Nash records the dark consequences of not doing so, especially when there is a serial killer running amok. Was the accident that prevented a staff member from attending work really just an accident? Isn't it a little too convenient when a stranger appears from nowhere and offers to fill in for them? Don't be fooled!

Selling's Murder

A fundamental part of working in retail is dealing with customers. They are an essential cog in the shopping machine – but wouldn't it be so much easier without them? Take your eyes off them for a second, due to a distraction or a loss of concentration, and they're messing with your stock, pilfering and worse. Here is an example of what could happen:

Case study: *The Gift Shop*
Author: Charlotte Armstrong
Date: 1966
Retail context: Airport gift shop
Consequences of not keeping an eye on customers:
A private eye, who has been stabbed during a flight, is able to leave a dying message inside one of the piggy banks the gift shop stocks. The shop assistant Jean Cunliffe unwittingly sells a trayful of them to a customer. Many

people are after that piggy bank, and the race is on for Jean to find it before the others do. If she had spotted what the private eye was up to, she could have spared herself a hazardous treasure hunt.

Those working in retail should also be aware of the signs that something suspicious is going on at their shop:

- ❑ Secretive and shady characters visit your shop after closing hours, late at night.
- ❑ Your employer refuses to sell specific items in the shop but won't explain why.
- ❑ Your employer openly admits that they are adopting a false name for their business.

If your workplace meets all three criteria, some criminal activity is potentially taking place. You can, like Thomas Melsonby,[16] try to hand in your notice, but there is the possibility they might reject it. If you are not killed for knowing too much, there is a high chance you will need to do some amateur sleuthing to prove your innocence of another crime.

Flirting with the boss to gain the upper hand in a promotions battle might seem like a good idea if you become their favourite, but this plan is not fool-proof. You may still be overlooked for the new role, your underhand tactics will encourage backbiting and jealousy from your colleagues, and they might even lead to your death. Christianna Brand's *Death in High Heels* shows how Miss Doon learnt this lesson the hard way. Oxalic crystals on curried rabbit, anyone? Conversely, while you might not want to become too friendly with your boss, you also don't want to antagonise them. Performing unflattering impersonations of their spouse is definitely something to avoid.[17]

Murder by the Book

Unfortunately, if you work in a bookshop you need to expect corpses around every corner, as murderers seem to gravitate towards this retail location. Alice Tilton records the surprise of Dot Peters, a bookshop owner, at the criminal activities her business experiences: 'racketeers, burglaries, stolen cars, bullets, murders, book thieves! And she had thought that the life of a second hand bookstore proprietress would be as dull and dusty as the second hand books!'[18]

Expensive and rare items are one of the reasons criminals are drawn to bookshops, so always keep such books under lock and key, as they can be a motive for robbery and murder. There were several such cases recorded in the 1930s in the UK, the United States and Italy.[19] Sometimes it is simply the book that is valuable in and of itself,[20] but on other occasions a book may be killed for, if it contains information on how to locate a more important prize. W. F. Harvey documents an unusual instance of this in *The Mysterious Mr Badman*, in which several people are prepared to steal and even kill for a particular book which has an MP's compromising letter inside it.

Before you give up on your dream of working in a bookshop it should be noted that in the classic crime universe, such jobs command high wages, if John Rutherford's bookshop is anything to go by:

> *At the end of the first month, I doubled his salary – George would never admit that he worked for such common things as wages – and at the end of the third month, I doubled it again.*[21]

If I was George, though, I would be working with one eye looking over my shoulder in case anyone tried to murder me for my job! Another perk to be considered is that if you are investigating a bookshop murder, you are entitled to do some book browsing and even leave a note so that the heirs to the business know you want to buy some of their stock. Or at least, that is what Max Boyle in R. T. Campbell's *Bodies in a Bookshop* thinks: 'I did not see why I should allow the death of the old proprietor to interfere with the growth of my library.'[22]

KEY SKILL

Fatal Purchase

Nowadays we can complete our lunch-hour shopping from the comfort of our seat with a few clicks, but in the classic crime universe all lunchtime shopping must be done on foot. Always scrutinise the mannequins in the shop windows, just in case they're real bodies,[23] while keeping an eye on your fellow shoppers when walking down crowded streets (especially at Christmas). Congested streets may provide a good opportunity to commit murder. Craig Rice chronicles such a case in *The Wrong Murder,* and while you might think the extra people in the area would increase the number of useful witnesses available, sadly they do not. In the world of classic crime, a dim view is taken of witnesses if Clifford Witting's opinion is anything to go by: 'Average Englishmen, he knew, had as keenly developed powers of observation as a congregation of turnips.'[24]

Finally, impulse buying is not recommended, particularly in shops that stock second-hand products, unless you have thoroughly checked the item over for signs of involvement in criminal activities. There may be others who are keen to gain possession of the item. In the case of Nurse Hinde, her impulse buy was a ring in a junk dealer's shop, but the trouble and near-death experiences it caused her were certainly not worth it![25]

She Fell among Actors

Some of us dream of seeing our names in lights, but how can you avoid the many dangers of working in the performing arts? Our CCSRU has put together a step-by-step plan to help you survive the five stages of performing arts.

Stage 1: Accepting the right job opportunities

While it is well known that actors eschew saying the word 'Macbeth' in the theatre, it is also the case that this play is notorious for encouraging real-life murder, so it is best circumvented, as is *Romeo and Juliet*.[26] Caution is advised when accepting jobs to conduct musical performances. In the classic crime universe conductors are surprisingly unpopular with orchestra members and audiences alike, as Sebastian Farr attests in *Death on the Down Beat*. Obnoxious behaviour was very much a key factor in the murder of Sir Noel Grampian. But if you are determined to conduct, we recommend some bulletproof glass. Taking on an understudy role is also risky, especially as you are required to act in lieu of someone else at short notice. This can cause havoc with a prospective killer's plans, and you may be in danger of being erroneously murdered.

Stage 2: Rehearsals

John Bude in *Death in White Pyjamas* advocates only taking part in rehearsals at the theatre, rather than those at country house retreats, as the line between the social and the professional can begin to blur and cause problems. Bude also stresses the need to keep your distance from troublemakers among the cast, who may use your personal information against you. Margery Allingham supports these measures in *Dancers in Mourning*, which charts the lengths actors may go to express their jealousy or irritation. Poison pen letters, vandalism and spikes concealed within greasepaint are all to be watched out for.

Stage 3: Backstage

Before stage props are used, it is important to double check they have not been tampered with. This is especially applicable if the prop is a gun. Are those bullets blanks or genuine? The fatal consequences of not checking are well documented in Ngaio Marsh's *Enter a Murderer*. Marsh has recorded many theatre murders; further findings from these case studies include:

- ❑ Urging all pianists to examine their instruments before use, to ensure they have not been rigged with a gun that fires when a certain key is struck.[27]

- ❑ Recommending that actors insist with management on the use of electric rather than gas heating in their dressing rooms.[28]

Although you might want some peace and quiet backstage before you are due to perform, be wary of the fact your isolation will make it easier for a would-be murderer to pick you off, something violinist Lucy Carless discovered to her cost.[29]

Stage 4: During the performance

Dodging death backstage is one thing, but the danger is not over when you are on stage. Your audience provides no immunity to murder, which is supported by ample case studies across a range of performing arts roles. Here are some further reading suggestions, depending on your job role:

Theatre actor: Alan Melville's *Quick Curtain*, E. and M. A. Radford's *Who Killed Dick Whittington?* and Helen McCloy's *Cue to Murder*
One danger specific to the theatre is the possibility the flying system above you has been tampered with; Agatha Christie and Ngaio Marsh both record murder cases in which this has happened.[30]

Ballet: Caryl Brahms and S. J. Simon's *A Bullet in the Ballet*

TV presenter: Patricia McGerr's *Death in a Million Living Rooms*

Radio play performer: Val Gielgud and Holt Marvell's *Death at Broadcasting House*

Stage 5: After the show

Before you congratulate yourself for having made it this far, don't become complacent and stay late after the performance has finished. Who knows who is lurking in the shadows, waiting to bump you off?[31] And when it comes to the critics, try to accept their reviews with good grace. Don't copy the example of Vladimir Stroganoff, who decides to drug a reviewer and write the review himself, after his attempts to bribe them fail. Ethically dubious and makes you look bad in the eyes of the police if the reviewer is then unfortunately murdered.[32]

One arena of performing arts which has not been discussed is the circus. This is a risky occupation, as the combination of a close working environment and murder weapons on hand makes it a job that can certainly be bad for your health. Both Alan Melville's *Death of Anton* and Nicholas Brady's *Fair Murder* evidence this danger. Melville's case study, along with E. C. R. Lorac's report, *Murder by Matchlight*, also further demonstrate the additional hazard that any specialist skills you have, such as knife throwing, will increase your chances of becoming a prime suspect, if a murder occurs.

Your daily toil at an end, you return home, as the fog is easing up. With a little extra money in your pocket, you're wondering if you should go out tonight and treat yourself. Surely, you think, the dangers have now passed. There's no need to heed the warning: Don't Go Out after Dark. But what dangers await you out there? Will there be death before dinner, or will it slowly dawn on you partway through that you are entertaining murder?

LESSON 4
Death Joins the Party

To stay in or go out. One of life's trickier choices. Even once you have decided to seek entertainment outside the home, where should you go? Options are plentiful, ranging from the cinema and the local tennis club to accepting party invitations or attending the local dance hall, if you really want to let your hair down.[1] Nevertheless, murderers never clock off, and your social activities could be the perfect opportunity they have been waiting for …

Death Steals the Show

Perhaps your first thought was to visit the cinema. Where else can you find Clark Gable, Bette Davis, Marlene Dietrich and many others all under one roof? But in the classic crime universe, should you be worried about a knife in the back when sitting in a darkened auditorium? The CCSRU has uncovered some case studies to help shed a light on the pros and cons of going to the cinema …

Con no. 1

Murder within the auditorium does happen, but only rarely. You are more likely to be murdered when attending the theatre,[2] especially if you have booked a seat in a box. Who knows what will come creeping up behind you? While in a theatre box it is recommended to choose a chair near a wall, at the cinema it is advisable to pick a seat with an empty space either side of it and remain seated until the lights are restored. After all, there is still the occasional occurrence of cinema murder, as Agatha Christie can attest.[3]

Risk to life: Low–Medium (depending on which venue you attend)

Pro no. 1

Unlike theatre productions, film viewings largely preclude audience participation. Audience participation can not only be embarrassing but in some cases can also result in your death. A. E. Martin records such an instance in *Death in the Limelight*, in which an audience volunteer is stabbed during a hypnotism act.

Con no. 2

Perhaps a greater risk than being killed in a cinema is being so influenced by your film choices that you use them as a basis for your real-life decision-making. Anne Beddingfeld was one such cinemagoer. Christie charts the many dangers she faces in *The Man in the Brown Suit*, and all her near-death experiences stem from her decision to go off to South Africa to solve a London Underground murder – a decision fuelled by her many viewings of *The Perils of Pamela*.

Risk to life: Low–High (depending on how easily influenced you are by films and by what film genres you watch)

Con no. 3

There is one very niche corner of the classic crime universe which blames cinemas for making audiences incapable of enjoying school dance performances. This corner can be found in Josephine Tey's *Miss Pym Disposes*, which suggests that people were prevented from appreciating the pupils' performing because their cinema viewing had raised their standards too high.

Risk to life: Low (there are no recorded cases of anyone dying due to boredom at a school performance)

Pro no. 2

There is some evidence to suggest that certain films could help solve crimes. This research comes from Francis Vivian, who records in *The Laughing Dog* how one police sergeant felt that watching Disney films was a good way to relax when working on a case, as this period of relaxation aided the thinking process. Moreover, the sergeant mentions that a Mickey Mouse cartoon enabled his superior Inspector Knollis in solving one case.

Invitation to Murder

There are two sides to parties: one side plans and hosts and the other attends them as guests. Both groups have different dangers to be mindful of.

Prevention is better than a cure, and this certainly applies to party planning. The more pitfalls you can remove at this stage the better, and this begins with the guest list.

Guest list blacklist

If hosting a party, never invite:

- ❑ **Anyone who will want to extract money from you, and who may become violent if you refuse**
  Source: Anne Meredith's *Portrait of a Murderer*

- ❑ **Ex-lovers and their wives**
  Source: Mary Fitt's *Three Sisters Flew Home*

- ❑ **Anyone who has got away with murder in the past, especially if they have an inkling you know this**
  Source: Christie's *Cards on the Table*

- ❑ **Groups of family members who loathe one another**
  Source: Georgette Heyer's *Envious Casca*

- ❑ **Business rivals**
  Source: Ngaio Marsh's *Death and the Dancing Footman*

- ❑ **Plastic surgeons and patients whose treatments they botched**
  Source: Ngaio Marsh's *Death and the Dancing Footman*

While it feels good to be included in social occasions, accepting certain invites could cause you a lot of distress or even shorten your lifespan. We urge you to regretfully decline any of the following invitations to…

Haunted houses, especially if it is Hallowe'en
Further reading: Gerald Verner's *They Walk in Darkness* and John Dickson Carr's *Castle Skull*. The terror produced by the haunted house in *Castle Skull* is aided by its magician owner, who, Carr reports, 'spent a year transforming that weird ruin into a place of the nightmare … Every trick of his ingenuity was expended on devices to make the average man fear for his wits.'[4]

Reunions
Further reading: Ethel Lina White's *The Man Who Loved Lions*, which also notes that reunions taking place at night and/or at a private zoo are even more perilous.

Country house parties, when the host claims to have known your family, yet you have never heard of them
Further reading: Alan Melville's *Weekend at Thrackley*

Parties hosted on islands

Further reading: Anthony Boucher's *The Case of the Seven Sneezes*. Boucher points out the high risk of a criminal destroying the only means of transportation. If you are still keen on attending, bringing an inflatable dinghy in your handbag might be a good idea.

Parties hosted on April Fool's Day

Further reading: Frances and Richard Lockridge's *Curtain for a Jester*. April Fool's Day is all about pranks, and we all know how practical jokes in the classic crime universe can turn from laughter to murder.

KEY SKILL

Who Steals My Name?

What do you do when someone is impersonating you or someone you know? Here are five top tips for handling impostors.

- Not every impostor is after an inheritance, so it is important to uncover why someone is pretending to be you. Sometimes it can be possible to take them aside to ask them this, but you might not want to delay this action, as you never know when they might be murdered.
  Source: Helen McCloy's *Alias Basil Willing*

- ☛ Practise being observant of other people, noting small details about them, such as boils. This will help you to identify if someone tries to impersonate them later.
  Source: Christie's *They Came to Baghdad*

- ☛ Until you have proof that the person is an impostor, out for financial benefits, remember to act politely, as if others have been taken in by them, you may become alienated from the group if you are too hostile. You also don't know how the impostor might retaliate.
  Sources: Josephine Tey's *Brat Farrar* and Georgette Heyer's *Penhallow*

- ☛ Try to avoid letting your emotions cloud your judgement when assessing the authenticity of a potential legatee to your will. Ask a disinterested party to help you.
  Source: Julian Symons's *The Belting Inheritance*

- ☛ If someone's identity is in doubt, do not alert them to the fact that you possess information that calls their claim into question: if there is a lot of money involved, they might decide to eliminate you.
  Source: Patricia Wentworth's *The Traveller Returns*

The Party Killer

Having chosen a safe party to attend, there is still further preparation you can do beforehand to minimise fatalities. Certain parties, such as debutante balls, are more important than others, and there may be additional pressure to look your best. However, be careful what slimming products you use, as some may have deadly consequences.[5] For some people, getting ready for a party is a social activity and they enjoy giving other people makeovers. But if there is a killer on the loose it is probably not wise to tie your makeover participant to a chair as a practical joke, especially if you then forget to untie her.[6] Vincent Starrett, author of *The Great Hotel Murder*, would also recommend taking a lifejacket if your party is taking place on water, even if it clashes with your outfit. Accessories can make an outfit, but be warned that wearing expensive, priceless jewellery to parties comes with risks. Even if you are not killed for the items, they still have a tendency to wander.[7]

A common murder method deployed at social gatherings is the poisoned drink, so this is something you should be especially mindful of. Look at this scene and see if you can spot the opportunities there are to add a lethal dose to someone's beverage.

Once you are ready, read the answers below, garnered from the CCSRU's archives.

Opportunity no. 1

Always watch your drink. You may want to join in with the dancing, go and chat with someone, or even use the bathroom, but before you leave your drink you need to finish it – or get a fresh one later. The classic crime universe is littered with people who wish they had followed this advice.

Case study: Frances and Richard Lockridge's *A Pinch of Poison*

Opportunity no. 2

Always make sure you pick up the correct glass, as choosing someone else's drink may mean you save their life at the cost of your own, if a killer was targeting them instead.

Case studies: Christie's *Sparkling Cyanide* and *Curtain*

Opportunity no. 3

Unplanned distractions such as a telephone call or a dropped glass, as well as orchestrated diversions, like small acts of arson, power cuts and dimmed lights, can be used to the would-be murderer's advantage, if they make you take your eyes from your glass or cause you to leave the room entirely.

Case studies: Christie's 'Yellow Iris', Belton Cobb's *The Poisoner's Mistake* and J. Jefferson Farjeon's *The Oval Table*

Opportunity no. 4

It may seem anti-social but be wary of accepting other people's drinks, especially if your own has been knocked over. Maybe they are being kind, but there is also the possibility that the fresh drink has a hefty dose of poison in it. Your suspicions should be further aroused if the person offering their drink to you was also involved in your drink being spilt.

Case study: Josephine Pullein-Thompson's *Gin and Murder*

Even if your drink is not laced with poison, it is still an unwise decision to overdrink in the classic crime universe. Not only may you commit the social faux pas of falling asleep in your host's study, but you may become an important witness for a murder, yet not remember enough to ensure your survival.[8] Or worse still, someone might use your drunken state to their own advantage by framing you for their crime.[9]

Danger does not just lie in the comestibles at a social gathering, but potentially in the entertainment too. Participating in a party game can leave you dicing with death! Games provide too many opportunities for committing murders and often involve a period of darkness, meaning no one has a reliable alibi. Two of the most lethal games to play are …

Hide and seek

You might think you are a pro at this game, able to hide in the smallest of spaces, but what if someone locks you inside this killer hiding spot? In a remote location your cries for help will remain unheard, as you rapidly run out of oxygen.

Source: R. C. Ashby's *Death on Tiptoe*[10]

Murder game

When a fake murder to solve is planned as entertainment, you can guarantee someone will be tempted to add a real corpse to the game. Your chances of adding grizzly authenticity to the game are increased if the lights are turned off or if your hosts decide to include genuine murder weapons in the game.

Sources: Ngaio Marsh's *A Man Lay Dead*, Ellery Queen's 'The Dead Cat'[11] and Anthony Berkeley's *The Second Shot*

Finally, for hosts, here are three mistakes you can learn from:

Case study: *The Deadly Truth*
Author: Helen McCloy
Date: 1943
Victim: Claudia Bethune
What the victim did: Pranked her guests by drugging their drinks with a stolen truth drug. By the end of the night, she is brutally murdered.
What the victim should have done: Brought a game of Monopoly to play at the party instead.

Case study: *The Clock Strikes Twelve*[12]
Author: Patricia Wentworth
Date: 1944
Victim: James Paradine
What the victim did: Issued an unpleasant ultimatum at dinner, regarding stolen papers.
What the victim should have done: Alerted the police to the theft, before publicly revealing the loss.

Case study: *Sparkling Cyanide*[13]
Author: Agatha Christie
Date: 1945
Victim: George Barton
What the victim did: Decided to solve his wife's death by reconstructing the events running up to it.
What the victim should have done: Discussed his concerns with the police or a private detective so better safety measures could have been put in place.

Dressed to Kill

If you dread fancy dress parties, the advice below might give you the ammunition you need to boycott them for good. In short, fancy dress parties should be avoided at all costs. They have a magnetic attraction for prospective killers, and in the classic crime universe, the death of at least one guest is inevitable. This risk is heightened if the fancy dress theme is true crime murderers and victims.[14] Anthony Berkeley records one such case in *Jumping Jenny*, where the foolhardy host has even erected a fake gallows. You just know by the end of the night a real corpse will be found on it!

There are several reasons why fancy dress parties are so deadly. The first of these, pinpointed by Christie,[15] is the difficulty of identifying people correctly. It does not help that murderers on these occasions can be inclined to swap costumes to implicate others. This situation is exacerbated if guests are expected to wear identical costumes, an issue raised in *Death of a Doll* and *Death in Clairvoyance*, by Hilda Lawrence and Josephine Bell, respectively. Thirdly, fancy dress costumes often involve large amounts of fabric: one of Miss Marple's cold case successes demonstrates how useful this excess material can be for concealing a weapon.[16]

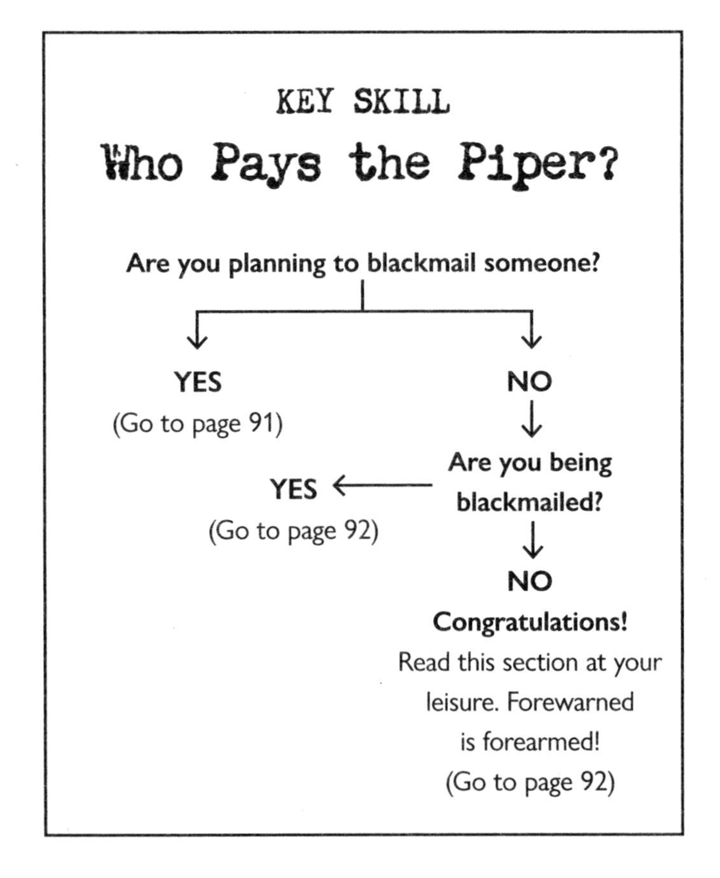

Four top tips for the successful blackmailer, or: How not to get murdered by your victims

- ☛ Don't invite your victims to your house for a visit.
  Source: Patricia Wentworth's *Wicked Uncle*

- ☛ Don't request free board and lodgings from your victim.
  Source: Peter Shaffer's *The Woman in the Wardrobe*

- ☛ Don't spend time regularly with your victim socially or share a commute with them.
  Source: E. and M. A. Radford's ***Death of a Frightened Editor***

- ☛ Put safeguards in place for collecting your money. Avoid isolated spots and meeting your prey alone.
  Source: Christie's ***Death on the Nile***

How not to deal with a blackmailer

As tempting as it is to bump off the person financially sucking you dry, we don't recommend this option. Are you sure you have identified the right person? Are you confident you can execute the task effectively, without being noticed? Cyril Hare charts the pitfalls of ignoring this advice in his short case study, 'Your Old Leech'.[17]

Going to the law is the safer option, as is leaving the police to trap the culprit. Learn from Lord Gospell's mistake.[18] He allowed the blackmailer to discover his intentions of identifying him for the purposes of prosecution, and naturally the guilty party decided to take preventive action..

Crime at Christmas

Christmas can be a very social time, with lots of parties and other activities to attend. However, it is also a time of arguments and tempers boiling over. To help you have a happy festive season the CCSRU has produced a catalogue of inventions to eradicate the more common Yuletide perils.

SORE THROAT NOISE SIMULATOR

This handy device is guaranteed to get you out of being strong-armed into door-to-door carol singing. Not only does this mean you get to stay cosy at home with the television, but it also provides a would-be killer with one less opportunity to eliminate you.

RRP: 13s. 9d.

This invention was inspired by Clifford Witting's *Catt Out of the Bag*.

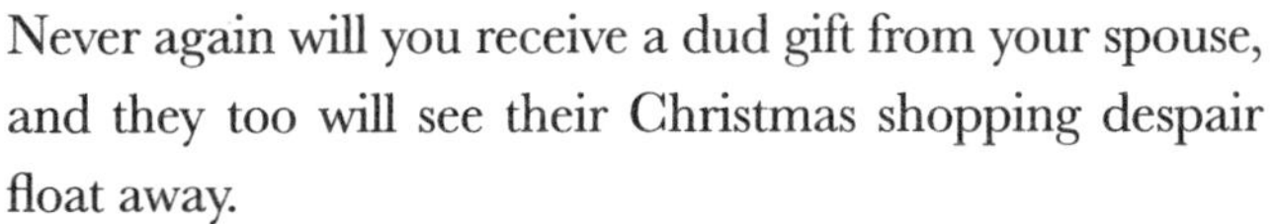

GOOD GIFT-FINDING GOGGLES

With the function to programme in your present preferences, these goggles are a relationship lifesaver. Never again will you receive a dud gift from your spouse, and they too will see their Christmas shopping despair float away.

RRP: £140

Customer review

This was my Christmas shopping experience before I owned these goggles: 'Trailing from shop to shop, I gaped in windows over the heads of those in front of me, but could hit upon no suitable present for my wife. In the end I bought her a hand-bag, which, if the colour was right (which was unlikely) and the shape acceptable (which was improbable), would form a pleasant addition to her wardrobe.'[19] Now, though, my shopping time is cut in half, and

I have much greater confidence in the purchases that I make. Worth every penny! (John Rutherford)

THE ORIGINAL SANTA KLAUS OUTFIT DESTROYER

While many have tried to create the perfect robotic demolisher of these outfits, none have surpassed the determination and high success rates of our canine operatives. They come in a range of sizes to meet individual household needs and are guaranteed to annihilate any Father Christmas attire in their vicinity.

RRP: £5–20 (depending on size and breed of operative)

Note to customers: Our canine operatives are not just for Christmas and must be cared for year-round. For best results avoid wearing any red clothing.

CCSRU MEMO

Re. Banning of Santa Klaus Costumes

We are aware that this invention may aggrieve some readers. To prevent sacks full of letters to our complaints department, we would like to outline the many dangers such outfits present:

Torturous wearing experience

Our unit has received countless reports of how uncomfortable these garments are to don. Clifford Witting documents such a case: 'I was suffocating. It clung to me, smothering my mouth and nostrils when I tried to breathe. My body and head were enveloped by the thick heavy folds. All around me were screaming voices, and the place was unbearably hot. I longed for the torment to end, but the shrieks and yells grew louder until my head swam.'[20]

Prime murder target

In the unit's archives there are many studies to support the theory of a strong correlation between being the person wearing the Santa Klaus outfit and being the person who gets murdered. Case studies include:

- ❑ Rupert Latimer's *Murder after Christmas*
- ❑ Mavis Doriel Hay's *The Santa Klaus Murder*
- ❑ Francis Duncan's *Murder for Christmas*
- ❑ Ngaio Marsh's *Tied Up in Tinsel*

Prime suspect

Conversely, if the Santa Klaus costume wearer is not the victim, there is a high chance of them being the guilty party. The crime might be the leaving of unpleasant gifts,[21] but it can also be one of murder. Whether you did the deed or not, if you are wearing such a festive outfit the police will immediately begin to suspect you. Researcher Fredric Brown notes that one reason killers use such clothing is because it is difficult to identify someone when wearing it, and at Christmas such a disguise is rarely questioned.[22]

PERSONAL PROPERTY PROTECTOR

Generally, it is inadvisable to wear expensive jewellery to a social occasion, but for those with plenty of bling, this restriction can be distressing. They want to show off their treasured items yet are fearful of losing them. Well fear no more! Heading up the avian division of the CCSRU are our personal property protector parrots. These keen-eyed birds are trained to be vigilant and will sound the alarm if anyone comes too close to your diamond necklace or valuable ring. Their portable size means they are easy to take to parties and they are comfortable in any social situation, having taken an extensive etiquette course.

RRP: £20–70 (depending on size and breed of operative)
This invention was inspired by G. K. Chesterton's 'The Flying Stars'.[23]

THE FAKE DRINK

This device was developed to reduce poisonings which occur during toasts. The fake drink looks like an ordinary glass, but inside it has a hidden layer. This clear glass layer partially contains a liquid the same colour as your preferred alcoholic beverage. When you are asked to raise a glass during a toast and drink, the liquid moving in the hidden layer simulates the act of drinking, when in reality the centre of your cup is bone dry.

RRP: 10s.

This invention was inspired by Cyril Hare's *An English Murder*.

SNOWMAN BODY DETECTOR

Are you tired of people leaving corpses in your snowmen? Are your children perpetually left in tears by the police smashing their creations to the ground in order to look for missing persons? If you answered yes to either of these questions, the snowman body detector is the device for you. The detector provides a non-invasive means of ascertaining if a body is inside your snowman, meaning empty snowmen are not unnecessarily ruined. The device also features an alarm to emit a loud noise if anyone comes close to your snow creation.

RRP: £74 19s. 9½d.

This invention was inspired by Nicholas Blake's *The Case of the Abominable Snowman*.

KEY SKILL

Death Is No Sportsman

The CCSRU often receives enquiries from the public on how to stay safe. Here is a selection of questions sent in, concerning personal safety when playing sport.

Q: Which sports should I avoid if I don't want to end up embroiled in a murder case or in a scenario where I must foil a villainous plot?
A: One sport you should steer clear of is golf. This activity has a track record of attracting criminal activity. If you are not coming across a corpse, like Bobby Jones,[24] you might uncover an espionage conspiracy,[25] and of course once you have discovered such an intrigue naturally you will feel obliged to thwart it, which is time-consuming and puts you in perilous situations. If you insist on playing golf, we strongly advise against personalising your golf balls, as they are an excellent way for someone to frame you for a crime. Gerald Verner records such a case in 'The Red Golf Ball'.[26]

Q: A rich elderly relative has made a new will in which I can only claim my inheritance if I successfully qualify for the Olympics in a given sport. What should I do?
A: As painful as it might seem, we recommend waiving all rights to the money. Gladys Mitchell's report, *The Longer Bodies*, supports this, detailing various people facing a similar set of circumstances. If you are unsuited to your selected sport the training will be gruelling, and there is also the chance of becoming a victim of a sport equipment-related murder.

Q: What measures can I take to ensure that my sporting equipment is not involved in criminal activity?
A: Firstly, you should keep all your equipment, such as cricket bats and bows and arrows, under lock and key when not in use, as that reduces its likelihood of being used as a murder weapon. If other people are bringing their own equipment this too should be securely stored.
Further reading: Carter Dickson's *The Skeleton in the Clock* and John Bude's *The Cheltenham Square Murder*

Secondly, if it is not possible to lock your equipment away securely, or too many people possess a key to that area, then before you or anyone uses your sport equipment, you must check that none of it has been tampered with. Criminals may tamper with equipment for the purposes of concealing valuable items[27] or may have the more serious intention of ending someone's life. Even leg pads for cricketers, items designed to prevent injury, can be manipulated to do the very opposite.[28]
Further reading: Josephine Tey's *Miss Pym Disposes*

Pondering your options and frowning at the rain which has begun to fall, you decide to save money for something bigger instead, like your next holiday. After all, you never know when you might want to get away for a bit. Life has been quite stressful lately, you reflect; you've definitely earned a break. But criminal intentions and murderous plans are not left at home when people go on holiday. There will be death among the sunbathers, and you will more than likely find a corpse in the guest suite. There's always room for murder. Time for your next lesson, so you can avoid taking a passport to oblivion or becoming the sunburned corpse …

LESSON 5
Murder Takes No Holiday

Whether you love city breaks, beach holidays, the fun-filled activities of Butlin's holiday camps[1] or prefer going off the beaten track, the world of classic crime has it all! But murder takes no break, so from the moment you begin planning your getaway, you must be on your guard.

The Best-Laid Plans

The first question to answer is: where shall I go? There are many ways to go about deciding your destination, yet some are more reliable than others:

Method 1: Blindly sticking a pin into a map
Potential issues: There is a high chance of sticking it in the middle of the sea, and if you are living in a classic

crime novel, the place you pin will invariably have a murder.
Case study: Delano Ames's *Death of a Fellow Traveller*
Reliability rating: Low

Method 2: Personal recommendations

Potential issues: Opinions vary on what good accommodation consists of. The quality of the hospitality may also have dipped since the recommender's visit. One woman ended up in a room with a hole in the ceiling – a hole which soon let in a downpour of rain. Even if she did bring a raincoat, she shouldn't be expected to wear it in bed!
Case study: Lenore Glen Offord's *The Nine Dark Hours*
Reliability rating: Varies from low to high depending on the person giving the recommendation.

Often, when going on holiday, you need to communicate with your accommodation in advance, whether you are staying with a friend or booking a hotel room. While spontaneity has its moments, it is important to adhere to this rule: always let people know when you are planning on arriving. Telegrams and letters can get lost in transit, but you should still be wary if someone (or their servants) claim they never received your message informing them of your arrival date. Is this a way of putting you off staying? If, like Catherine West, you are going to visit an infirm, richer and older relative, then it is more likely.[2]

As well as letting people know you are coming, you should also inform a family member or good friend of

COME TO DARTMOOR!

Do you love hiking in the fresh air, with wonderful panoramic views?

Do you have a strong sense of adventure?

Do you love birdwatching?

Do you love outdoor pursuits such as skiing?

If you answered yes to any of the above, Dartmoor is the holiday destination you have been waiting for!*

* Small print: Visitors should be aware there is usually at least one escaped convict on the moors at any given time. Nothing to worry about though, as they rarely have anything to do with the numerous murders which occur here.[3] You should not come if you have a fear of dogs, have avaricious heirs or are due a financial windfall.

your travel dates, in case problems arise. Failing to do this will delay any search for you if you are in danger, or if you have been killed, it can make it harder for the police to investigate your death. While you might avoid such a fate by the skin of your teeth, like Iris Carr,[4] you might not. Celebrities wishing to holiday away from the public gaze, as evidenced by Josephine Tey,[5] are more prone to this difficulty.

Delano Ames, who has chronicled the many perils of travelling, also advises avoiding the rookie error of delegating the task of making room reservations to an unreliable and forgetful third party. You might be dreaming of luxurious bedsheets and a warm bath, but could end up with an attic space and a camp bed if the essential booking has not been made.

If you are worrying about how to afford going on holiday, Jane and Dagobert Brown, as reported by Ames, recommend alternating between nights sleeping in high-end hotels and dining in the cheapest bistros, and days staying in the most economical hotels and eating in the priciest restaurants. However, Jane admits two downsides to the system: 'It is puzzling to doormen and waiters and it is practically impossible to dress for.'[6] Nevertheless, one suggestion we would discourage, even if your daughter is desperate to go on holiday to Egypt, is staying in a haunted house for six months. Even if all her friends are going, it is far too hazardous to undertake such a task. Spoiling your child in this instance may cost you your life![7]

Finally, last-minute changes can be unavoidable. An injury or problem at work may prevent someone from joining your holiday party. However, beware taking on board last-minute substitutes unless you know them very well. Carol Carnac chronicles the many inconveniences of harbouring a murderer in your group holiday, in her case study *Crossed Skis*.

KEY SKILL

Death Packs a Suitcase

Having decided on your destination, the next task is making sure you pack the right clothes.

- If you are using a mode of transport which is travelling through several countries, such as the Orient Express, remember to take clothing appropriate to all climates. Shorts and summer dresses may suit hot Turkish weather but if you end up stranded somewhere like Yugoslavia, due to huge snowfall, you will bitterly regret it if you haven't brought a jumper or two.

- Avoid paralysing overthinking and follow the simple rule that if in doubt, always take a raincoat (especially if you are holidaying in the UK).[8]

- While there is much to be said for minimalist packing, bear in mind that unexpected social occasions are possible. Anticipating this in your packing is desirable, unless you are happy to buy new clothes at your holiday destination. Harriet Vane found herself in such a situation while hiking. She preferred to pack light, prioritising comfort. 'Consequently, her luggage was not burdened by skin-creams, insect lotion, silk frocks, portable electric irons, or other impedimenta beloved of the "Hikers' Column".'[9] Yet a flurry of holiday clothes shopping must ensue when she is required to go on picnics and attend dances to solve a murder.

- ☛ If the person in charge of organising the holiday is prone to abruptly changing their mind, we recommend packing a wider style of clothes to suit all occasions. Frequent traveller Jane Brown learnt this lesson the hard way when she packed for a rustic working holiday in a remote French village, only to discover that her husband had decided to book an expensive hotel on the Promenade des Anglais.[10]

- ☛ A fishing net may seem like an unusual item to pack, but the classic crime universe is full of useful tips on how to make your own holiday accessories. Christianna Brand suggests you 'wash out the excess tar, stitch gay white bobbles round the edge and wear thrown carelessly over your shoulder with an outsize straw hat'.[11] However, check that your accessories are appropriate to the climate of your holiday destination. Making the same poncho out of a red chenille tablecloth is ill-advised if you are going to a hot country.

Death Flight

Flying has many advantages in the classic crime world. The comparatively shorter travel time means a potential murderer has fewer opportunities to enact any plans and there is less passenger mingling. However, necessity is the mother of invention, so here are some dangers you should be mindful of, culled from the CCSRU archives …

BOARDING PASS

Name: Christopher St John Sprigg
From: Baston Aero Club **To:** Sankport
Flight: Death of an Airman **Date:** 1934 **Seat:** 1A
Gate: 4 **Boarding time:** 14:30
Important tip: If you are in the unenviable position of having to confront a killer, avoid doing so on a plane, particularly if they are the one flying it.

BOARDING PASS

Name: Agatha Christie
From: Le Bourget Airfield, Paris **To:** Croydon
Flight: Death in the Clouds **Date:** 1935 **Seat:** 9
Gate: 10 **Boarding time:** 12:00
Important tip: A coat with a thick furry collar is a good murder deterrent.

BOARDING PASS

Name: Christianna Brand
From: London Club **To:** Milan
Flight: Tour de Force **Date:** 1955 **Seat:** 3C
Gate: 6 **Boarding time:** 09:45
Important tip: If you want your holiday friendships to start on the right foot, when experiencing flight anxiety, avoid moulting upon and invading the personal space of your fellow passengers. They too may be struggling to maintain their calmness.

BOARDING PASS

Name: Margaret Carpenter
From: Las Vegas **To:** New York
Flight: Experiment Perilous **Date:** 1943 **Seat:** 4D
Gate: 1 **Boarding time:** 12:00
Important tip: If someone strikes up a conversation with you during the flight and tells you a lot about themselves, you can be certain they will be murdered once they leave the plane! As the last person they intimately talked to, you are duty bound to do some amateur sleuthing into their death. So if you don't want your holiday scuppered, don't talk to anyone on the plane!

Sailor, Take Warning!

There is lots of fun to be had on nautical holidays: visiting exotic new places, plentiful catering and numerous activities on board to beat the holiday blues. However, if you don't want your vacation plans shipwrecked, you had best steer clear of the following hazards …

☛ **Arguments on the upper deck**
Why: If tempers are high there is the strong temptation for someone to push you overboard. This temptation is increased if there are no bystanders and visibility is poor.
Source: Josephine Bell's 'The Packet-Boat Murder'[12]

☛ **Flagrant people-watching**
Why: People watching is a fun hobby, but if you are too obvious about it, or are spotted writing notes about what you see, your fellow holidaymakers may develop murderous intentions towards you.
Source: Nicholas Blake's *The Widow's Cruise*

☛ **Ensnaring gossip**
Why: It is important to stay in the loop with ship gossip, but if you indulge in it too much then tensions can run high.
Source: Margot Neville's *The Hateful Voyage*

☛ **Onboard romances**

Why: There is an expectation to find love while on holiday, as evidenced by Suzanne Blair's comment that 'everyone gets engaged on board ship. There's nothing else to do.'[13] However, try to avoid those only seeking time-limited flirtations, if you are looking for more – and more importantly, steer clear of passengers who happen to be murderers.

Source: Stuart Palmer's *The Puzzle of the Silver Persian*

☛ **Solo day trips**

Why: Adventurous holidaymakers who decide to explore by themselves have a strong tendency to not return – alive.

Source: Freeman Wills Crofts's *Found Floating*

☛ **Lethal luggage**

Why: The passengers on board wearing the ceremonial swords may be innocently enough going to attend an annual Ancient and Respectable Rifleman encampment, but you know one of their weapons is going to fall into the hands of a murderer. We recommend changing ships before it is too late!

Source: Frances and Richard Lockridge's *Voyage into Violence*

Death Rides a Tandem

For some, cycling, camping and hiking holidays are the ideal, while for others they are a form of torture. If you fall into the latter camp, you may be wondering how you can get out of a gruelling mountainside cycling trip. Claiming you can't ride a bicycle is a risky excuse due to the unfortunate invention of the tandem bicycle, and if you are at the rear of such a contraption the scenery is not likely to vary. The back of the neck of the person in front tends to feature largely. Arguably a stronger reason for getting out of cycling in the world of classic crime is the potential for getting shot at and being more vulnerable to such an attack. Delano Ames records such a case in *Murder, Maestro, Please*. However, if you happen to be a crime writer then you may be doomed to the cycling holiday because, as Dagobert Brown says to his mystery writing wife, 'It's copy ... some day you'll be able to use it ... probably.'[14]

If you want to avoid fanning the flames of ardour your partner has for cycling and hiking, you need to ensure they don't encounter an even more enthusiastic fan. You can spot them in the following ways:

- They only pretend to read a book, earwigging so they can join in and extol the virtues of cycling.

- They exude a longing to tell you 'about methylated spirits, wearing three pairs of socks and putting soap in boots'.[15]

- There is a fanatical look in their eyes.

- They wear shorts regardless of the weather and may have cycling club badges sewn on to their clothes.

A beach camping holiday could be a happy compromise, but don't let anyone third wheel on your couple's getaway. If you neglect to do this and that person dies (of natural causes, one hopes), don't try to conceal them within your car to get back across the border into your own country. And if you do manage to do this, don't leave your car unattended. No one likes to play hide and seek with a corpse! Ann and Toby can attest to the headaches this situation causes.[16]

Murder Is a Package Deal

Package holidays take the hassle of planning a trip off your shoulders and can be great for those who dislike holidaying alone. However, you must be prepared for all kinds of travellers. In *Tour de Force*, which focuses on an Italian package holiday, Christianna Brand found the following types:

- 'Refined ones looking down upon the jolly ones and hoping they wouldn't whip out funny hats and shame them at the advertised "first class hotels"

- Inexperienced ones who never could make out whether you called this place Mill-an or Mil-ann

- Experienced ones who fazed them all by calling it Milarno

- Robust ones who drank water out of taps and confounded the experienced ones by not going down with bouts of dysentery

- Anxious ones who refused all shellfish, raw fruit and unbottled beverages and went down with dysentery before they had even started.'[17]

Which one sounds most like you?

Holiday affairs can liven up a long vacation. Keen social commentator Jane Brown corrects her husband who disagreed:

> *Women with reliable husbands in distant lands and fascinating young French composers madly in love with them on the spot do not get bored. They may get into emotional difficulties, they may get their hearts torn asunder, they may even get mildly blackmailed. But they do not get bored.*[18]

Jane importantly notes the danger of being vulnerable to blackmail if you start a holiday love affair, and we also warn you to be wary of choosing the wrong partner. It is simpler for them to bump you off if you organise a private rendezvous with them, as Christie's report, *A Caribbean Mystery*, attests.

When it comes to booking a hotel room there are several factors to consider. Do you want one with a view? The whole family crammed into one room, or a separate room for the kids? Another factor is bathroom facilities. Always aim for an en suite, but if this is not possible you need to think carefully about which room you want.

Which is the best spot?

Without an en suite you need to schedule visits to the shared bathroom wisely, to sidestep long queues and the shortage of hot water. So should you go for a room as close as possible to the bathroom? Well, this depends on who you are holidaying with. If you are a parent with at least one sand- and ice cream-covered child then the closer the better, as John and Emery Bonett point out the reduced likelihood of you beating adults without dependants, in the race to the bathroom first, before the hot water runs out.[19]

However, bear in mind that by having the room closest to the bathroom, you may be subjected to sleepless nights if the plumbing is rather vocal. Inspector Minto fell foul of this predicament with pipes that 'gurgled and spluttered and generally behaved like Dante's Inferno all night'.[20] Adults without children may wish to avoid this problem and opt for a room further away.

If you find yourself with a less than ideal bedroom, be cautious about agreeing to swap with someone, as you may be spared the fate of no hot water, but instead may face the worse risk of a murder attempt intended for someone else.[21] Always remember to lock your room if you wish to avoid unpleasant surprises. As Nicholas Blake would tell you, nothing ruins a holiday quicker than finding a dead animal tucked up in your bed![22]

Package holidays can entail a lot of group activity, so it is understandable if you want some time alone. Nevertheless, isolation is not something we strongly recommend since it makes it easier for a killer to pick you off, which Mrs Boynton discovered to her cost.[23] Although group excursions are not without their risks. Always be on guard against falling rocks and shoves from behind, especially if walking high up or around ancient ruins. The CCSRU archive contains many case files on the matter, including Christie's *Death on the Nile* and *Nemesis*, as well as Patricia Highsmith's *The Two Faces of January*. Interestingly, how you wear your hair could save your life in such a situation. One woman who was pushed over a parapet avoided death as her long plaited hair became entangled in tree branches, giving her time to grab hold of something to stop her descent.[24]

Finally, in the event of going into the wrong bedroom accidentally, politely and quickly leaving the room is much better than hiding and waiting for the occupant to leave. You may be in for a long and uncomfortable wait; it will be even more awkward if you are discovered later – and there is always the chance you may face a firearm, if the occupant fears you are a burglar.[25]

The Riddle of the Sands

A day at the beach can be fun, but can also end in tears or worse, death, if you are not careful. Here are five tips on what not to do at the beach …

1 Do not take important evidence to the beach – or if you must, don't advertise the fact and then fall asleep. Don't be surprised if it is not there when you wake up!
Source: Jean Potts's *Death of a Stray Cat*

2 Do not fall asleep while sunbathing if you wish to avoid the classic holiday error of extremely painful sunburn.
Source: Juanita Sheridan's *What Dark Secret*

3 Avoid solo sea-bathing excursions, as they provide a would-be murderer with the opportunity to make your death look accidental.
Sources: C. H. B. Kitchin's *Death of His Uncle*

4 If you forget to take something on a picnic, don't return alone to collect the item, as this can be fatal.
Source: Carolyn Wells's *The Vanishing of Betty Varian*

5 Equally, if you notice someone has been gone a long time while fetching something, don't search for them on your own. Always take someone with you.
Source: Carolyn Wells's *The Vanishing of Betty Varian*

KEY SKILL

Death of a Fellow Traveller

Holidays can be worse than the first day of school when it comes to meeting new people and deciding how friendly to be. Take this quiz to see if you are prone to being too trusting or not trusting enough. Either extremity can leave you in danger in the classic crime universe.

Do you take people at face value?
A: Yes
B: No

Do you see your holidays as a chance for reinventing yourself, even if this means lying about who you are?
A: Yes
B: No

Are you susceptible to a pretty face?
A: Yes
B: No

Would you do a big favour for someone you had just met?
A: Yes
B: No

Are you more relaxed about bending the rules?
A: Yes
B: No

Have you been duped in the past by someone?
A: No
B: Yes

Do you prefer to play a lone hand?
A: No
B: Yes

Mostly As

You are prone to trusting others too much, which others can take advantage of. As Vande Lane points out: 'People are never exactly what they seem … especially on holiday … surrounded by people who don't know one. No give-away relatives, no childhood friends, no birth certificates, no diplomas, no marriage lines …'[26] In the world of classic crime it is foolhardy to not question what people say about themselves, especially if you hope to do some amateur sleuthing. Amateur sleuth status does not preclude you from becoming a murder victim. Star of the classic crime universe Miss Marple endorses this view, saying, 'I'm afraid that observing human nature for as long as I have done, one gets not to expect very much from it.'[27] She certainly wouldn't recommend being charmed or sweet-talked into doing a stranger a favour. Loaning someone money for ice cream is one thing, but if you are not vigilant you could be asked to do something illegal. Resist the temptation to do it simply because you think it will give you an ego boost, put a spark back into your marriage or give you a great holiday anecdote.[28]

Mostly Bs

You suffer from the opposite difficulty of trusting others too little. Miss Marple might have been cynical about human nature, but even she knew the value of accepting help from others. This is best seen in *Nemesis*, where at one point she summons help by using a whistle. Trusting others can be hard, especially when you have been hurt by someone close. But failing to do so could cost you dearly, as it did Hugh Everton in Margot Bennett's *The Widow of Bath*. He is determined to expose and break up a dangerous criminal gang. Yet he wishes to do so alone, which can only mean one thing: unplanned one-on-one combat. If you want to avoid near-strangulation and flesh wounds, we suggest you work alongside the police or find some trusted sidekicks.

Travel brochures are great for sorting out accommodation but are less useful when it comes to holiday romances. Alas, this is not the kind of thing you can plan, and a lot of on-the-spot decisions need to be made about whether a person is right for you. Even trying to meet new people at home is a difficult task. Love can be dangerous. How do you know that they are really interested in you and aren't just eyeing up your life savings? After all, you can't avoid the bathroom for the entire relationship …

LESSON 6

Romance in the First Degree

To love and be wise is the goal, but all too often in the classic crime universe the result is to love and to perish. So how can you sidestep such a fate? It all starts with that first encounter …

Meeting Trouble

How do you prefer to meet new people? An introduction by a friend? A chance encounter? Greater social freedom can give you more opportunities to meet someone, but what safety nets does it provide? Anthony Gilbert's Mass Observation report, *She Shall Die*, includes one participant who thought 'the Victorians had quite a lot of sense on their side',[1] in using references to vet newcomers. But since references are unlikely to make a comeback on the social scene, use the questions below to determine which classic crime love scenario you are most likely to face …

1. Do you prefer to be spontaneous?

Yes (go to question 2)
No (go to question 4)

2. Have you been told you are over-confident in your ability to judge others?

Yes (see result 1)
No (go to question 3)

3. Would an awkward first meeting hinder you in developing a relationship with someone?

Yes (see result 2)
No (see result 3)

4. Are you fed up with the mundaneness and pressures of your everyday life?

Yes (see result 4)
No (go to question 5)

5. Are you too busy to find love?

Yes (see result 5)
No (go to question 6)

6. Do you struggle with unrequited love?

Yes (see result 6)
No (go to question 7)

7. Conversely, do you find having too many suitors a hassle?

Yes (see result 7)

No (see result 8)

RESULT 1

If you make decisions hastily and don't often seek the advice of others, you have the potential for following in the footsteps of Victoria Jones. She had 'no inhibitions about making friends with strange young men in public places. She considered herself an excellent judge of character.'[2] Based on this self-confidence she rashly decided to follow a man she met once in a park, all the way to Baghdad. Yet this seemingly instant attraction led Victoria down a treacherous path, its danger heightened by impaired judgement.

RESULT 2

If you said yes to this question then Harriet Vane certainly knows how you feel, as she meets Lord Peter Wimsey, her future husband, for the first time while on remand. Yet past hurts, mistrust and the burden of gratitude mean their relationship takes some time to blossom.

RESULT 3

Not every awkward moment has to put a relationship on ice, though, if it is one you can laugh about afterwards. George Harmon Coxe's case study, *Murder with Pictures*, proves this point as a married couple, Joyce and Kent Murdock, meet for the first time when she hides in his shower while trying to evade a pursuing policeman. Unfortunately, Kent Murdock is using the shower at the time …

RESULT 4

Perhaps for a long time financial insecurity has meant you needed to concentrate on earning money, and at long last you can finally relax. Or can you? Ethel Lina White would suggest not, as her case study *Step in the Dark* reveals the jeopardy Georgia Yeo puts herself and her children in, when she decides to throw caution to the wind and grasp the glamorous life Count Gustav is offering her. Yet his charm conceals a diabolical plan, leaving her fighting for her life. White notes that this danger is more likely to occur if you are a thriller writer.

RESULT 5

If you're a working single parent, you might feel like you haven't got time to join a hobby group or go on dates due to all your commitments. So why not delegate the task of finding a new partner to your children? Craig Rice reports favourable results in *Home Sweet Homicide*. However, if your kids are not quite so successful in finding you love, take crime writer June Wright's advice and start a career in writing mystery novels to divert any desires for infanticide.

RESULT 6

It's not pleasant when you are intensely attracted to someone and they don't feel the same way, but it is important to avoid continuing to give any unwanted attention, as this can leave you in a vulnerable position if that person is then murdered.[3]

RESULT 7

While it can be flattering to have multiple suitors, it can also be quite stressful if you are unable to make your mind up, or cannot successfully push back against a suitor pressing for an answer. Like Hilary Fenton, backed into a corner, you may face the options of being tempted to acquiesce – or to lash out.[4]

RESULT 8

Alternatively, you might enjoy having lots of admirers, and what could make it more fun than a treasure hunt, in which the winner receives your hand in marriage? That is what Jo Fontyne thought until the dead bodies started turning up![5] Perhaps it is not such a good idea to make a game out of love after all.

Finally, if you are still wondering how best to judge someone's character, Nap Lombard's case study, *Murder's a Swine*, includes this nugget of advice: 'You could tell a man's character by the state of his waste-pipe.'[6] Make of that what you will!

KEY SKILL

The Fatal Flirt

The Classic Crime School of Flirting Course Registration

Flirting 101

This is a great beginner's course, covering core skills and basic errors. Here is what a previous attendee made of the course:

'Flirting 101 was just what I needed. I really struggled with knowing what to talk about when flirting. One time I even tried to flirt about central heating! Surely, I should have known such a relationship was doomed to failure! Now I am much more confident in what to flirt about.' Georgia Yeo.[7]

Tutor: Ethel Lina White

Time: Mondays 19:38

Flirting for Globetrotters

If you travel frequently for work or pleasure, you may be interested in discovering flirting tips from around the world. Some may surprise you, such as this one from China: attract others by knitting your eyebrows and looking like you have toothache.[8] You'll certainly get everyone's attention with that trick!

Tutor: James Norman

Time: Wednesdays 19:42

Genteel Flirting

This course teaches the subtle art of flirting. Do you want to be able to flirt 'so gracefully and delicately, to be able to break hearts just a little and not too much; and one's own heart not at all'?[9] Then sign up without delay!

Tutor: Christianna Brand

Time: Fridays 19:52

Flirt by Numbers

Do you struggle when confronted with maths-based flirting? Do you panic when someone asks: would you like to be the variable to my co-efficient? Well worry no more with this course, which is guaranteed to help you charm your way into the hearts of others with the allure of mathematical knowhow.

Tutor: Brian Flynn[10]

Time: Thursdays 19:28

Flirt Direct

Prefer the bold approach? Strongly believe that fair heart does not win fair lady, but lack confidence? Then this is the course for you. After a few sessions you will be able to say with suave conviction: 'If I knew you better Miss Ferris, I would show you my biceps.'[11]

Tutor: Lenore Glen Offord
Time: Tuesdays 19:41

We would advise you to be wary that no one is flirting with you in order to:

- Pump you for information regarding your employer. Amateur and police detectives are both prone to this annoying tendency and are not above proposing to you, if it will further their case. If you work in service, you are more likely to encounter this problem.[12]
- Camouflage their own criminal activities.
- Gain financially from you.
- Gain an upper hand over you.[13]

Conversely, if you are planning on doing some sleuthing which requires flirting, but you fear seduction, we recommend the following:

- Disable the radio and record player so you cannot be asked to dance.

- ☛ Ensure that you have control of the overhead lighting, so no one can unexpectedly dim the lights.

- ☛ Always leave a clear path to the nearest exit. Make sure there is no furniture in the way.

This advice is brought to you by Ludovic Travers, whose sleuthing exploits are chronicled by Christopher Bush. He suffers a close shave with this dilemma in his case entitled *Cut Throat*.

Death Makes a Date

You might now be armed with new flirting tips, but there are still other obstacles to avoid on the dating scene. For example, did you know that your suitability as a mate might be judged according to your ability to play bridge? Deficiencies in this department may lead to you being given the elbow, like Charles Venables.[14]

It can be difficult to know who to date or go on to marry, but a good rule of thumb, in the classic crime universe, is that you regularly exchange sarcastic remarks with one another, with perhaps brief moments of vulnerability. This is especially likely to be the case if you have had a previous history with the person or find yourself in the corner of the classic crime universe governed by Conyth Little. However, be careful you don't mistake dismissive or insulting comments for flirting. George Templeton comes a cropper when he tries to save the life and win the heart of Susan Blake. He ignores the warning signs, such as when she calls him 'the most incompetent spy' and the 'biggest fool in Scotland'.[15] If you find yourself in a similar situation to George (uncovering a group of criminals making weapons, while on a golfing holiday), we recommend that if you do fall in love with the criminal mastermind's daughter, check if she needs saving – and whether she wants saving by you.

Choosing where to go on your date is an important decision, and in the world of classic crime there is always the additional burden of corpses appearing at inopportune moments. Christianna Brand reports one case in *Death of Jezebel* where a courting couple pick the wrong bush to smooch under, finding themselves in very close proximity to a dismembered body. Unsurprisingly, they 'never felt quite the same towards one another again'.[16]

DATING CHECKLIST

Here are some signs that dating someone is not going well:

- ❑ You don't agree on your core values. When you disagree, the other person reacts badly, and they become distant and are tempted to be unfaithful.[17]

- ❑ The other person is prone to complaining during dates, making a nuisance of themselves with the waiting staff. You have to change seats at least once in a restaurant.[18]

- ❑ Conversation is one-sided and consists of extended monologues. The topics chosen to be talked about, by the other person, are never of interest to you.[19]

- ❑ The person you are dating frequently prioritises other activities over spending time with you.[20]

- ❑ The other person's brand of compliments is of the negative variety – they point out, for example, how you don't look as good as you normally do.[21]

Finally, we urge you to be honest when dating, as in the classic crime universe, deceit in this area can be fatal. Creating a fake dating profile might seem like a fun idea to amuse you and your friends, but not everyone handles rejection well: things could turn violent if they want revenge, as Sophie Tate learnt to her cost.[22]

Engaged to Murder

So you've found the person you want to spend the rest of your life with: how do you go about proposing to them? Alan Melville's *Weekend at Thrackley* demonstrates how to propose with panache:

Step 1: Ensure all villains have been thwarted, stolen property has been restored and any outstanding murders have been solved.

Step 2: Obtain an open-top sports car and offer to take the other person to their intended destination.

Step 3: Drive using one arm, while the other arm is draped around the shoulders of the other person. Make sure you don't muddle up which arm you use for each task!

Step 4: Adopt an artfully casual manner when you propose. You can use these lines as a template: 'There was one thing I wanted to ask you, though … what the devil was it, now? ... Oh, yes, I know – will you marry me, Mary?'[23] Don't forget to change the name, unless you happen to be proposing to someone called Mary! Remember to be direct when proposing, as too much conversational meandering – such as 'I was wondering if we could sort of … well, knock around together – see the sights, do a few shows and all that … but I mean … er … officially'[24] – may make it hard for the other person to realise that is what you are doing.

Step 5: Once your proposal has been accepted, kiss your fiancée, but only if you're proficient at driving. Try to keep one eye on the road to avoid obstacles such as chickens.

It is important to be honest during the engagement process, about yourself and your past experiences, as otherwise – if murder strikes – your partner may entertain grave suspicions about you. This inevitably places a lot of strain on the relationship, as Dick Markham describes: 'The main thing was to get rid of these cobwebs of suspicion, these ugly clinging strands that wind into the brain and nerves until you feel the spider stir at the end of every one of them.'[25]

You should also be aware that if you become engaged to a detective it is possible you will be roped in to do some physically demanding undercover work. When Inspector Vane's fiancée said yes, she may not have realised this would necessitate her taking on the role of a maid to solve one of his cases.[26] Using an engagement as a sleuthing ruse is not a tactic we would advise deploying, owing to the emotional distress caused. However, if you are adamant on using it, best wear your old clothes, as there is a high chance of an involuntary river immersion.[27]

Honeymoon with Death

In the classic crime universe, where murder is common, it is important to not rush into matrimony, as when crises occur you may struggle to trust your spouse. Conyth Little recorded such a case in *The Black Honeymoon*. Did Ian just marry Miriel to prevent her from marrying his uncle? Or did Miriel murder Ian's uncle so he couldn't change his will? If you are not careful, mistrust can have fatal consequences in a relationship, as Agatha Christie attests in 'Philomel Cottage'.

If you are soon to be a bride, these two case files could help prevent you making similar mistakes before and during your wedding day.

Case study: *Hasty Wedding*
Author: Mignon G. Eberhart
Date: 1937
Bride: Dorcas Whipple
What the bride did: Before rushing into a marriage of convenience, she visits her ex-lover the night before the wedding.
Consequences: The next day her ex-lover is said to have committed suicide, and soon after she is married, her husband whispers: 'I know you killed him.' Dorcas soon faces a murder charge.
What the bride should have done: Stayed at home and indulged in a fun recreational activity.

Case study: *The Wedding Guest Sat on a Stone*
Author: Richard Shattuck
Date: 1940
Bride: Sue Grant
What the bride did: Drank so much alcohol that she couldn't find her way back to the hotel's bridal suite.
Consequences: Sue enters the wrong room and gets into the wrong bed. Oh, did I mention the bed had a corpse in it?
What the bride should have done: Reined in her alcohol consumption a little, or got someone to escort her back to her room.

HONEYMOON DESTINATION CHECKLIST

When deciding where to go on your honeymoon, try to avoid …

❑ **Gangsters**

Why? Unsurprisingly, death is more likely to ensue with gangsters in the vicinity. Relaxing days by the pool are liable to be ruined by having to fight bad guys, and if you are putting them under surveillance leg cramp is inevitable, if you are hiding in the shrubbery for long.

Source: George Harmon Coxe's *The Barotique Mystery*

❑ **Relatives' houses**

Why? This might seem like a sensible option, as it means free accommodation, but it is guaranteed to be filled with other relatives who you weren't expecting to be there, and it won't be long until a corpse shows up.

Source: Conyth Little's *The Black Honeymoon*

❑ **Houses with corpses in the cellar**

Why? Although solving a murder can be an effective relationship-building exercise, it can cause additional strain, mess and inconvenience, particularly if you have had a long drive to the destination.

We recommend getting a local person to thoroughly search the property before you arrive.
Source: Dorothy L. Sayers's *Busman's Honeymoon*

KEY SKILL

Compliments of a Fiend

Giving backhanded compliments is a key mistake to avoid. Yet seemingly not everyone has found this an easy rule to follow in the classic crime universe. Below are our four Worst Compliment Competition entrants. How many of these have you experienced? And which do you think would be the worst to receive?

Entrant no. 1: Cyril
Compliment context: His girlfriend submitted his entry.
Compliment entry: 'Cyril's compliments are of a negative kind. He tells me if my colour isn't as good as usual or that he prefers my hair done the other way.'[28]

Entrant no. 2: Jane Marple
Compliment context: Miss Marple is reflecting on a woman whose life she saved in a previous case.
Compliment entry: 'A very nice woman. The kind that would so easily marry a bad lot. In fact the sort of woman that would marry a murderer if she were given half a chance.'[29]

Entrant no. 3: Sherlock Holmes
Compliment context: Holmes is addressing his sidekick Dr Watson.
Compliment entry: 'It may be that you are not yourself luminous, but you are a conductor of light. Some people without possessing genius have a remarkable power of stimulating it.'[30]

Entrant no. 4: Mona Brandon
Compliment context: Mona is discussing the stock of Jean Abbott's shop.
Compliment entry: 'I'm going to give your jewellery-stuff as Christmas presents … It looks like junk, but that's the style now.'[31]

Married into Murder

Marriage is like looking after a plant. Continued care and attention are required to keep it healthy. One sign your marriage is not healthy is if you can't tell if your spouse's declaration of love is 'referring to [you] or to the furnishings'.[32]

It is also wise not to over-compliment other women, even if they're from your past, as you never know when you are going to bump into them next – or maybe you do if you're Dagobert Brown, who decides to take his wife on a direct drive to Detroit via New Mexico ... It's a remarkable coincidence that Miranda Ross, one of 'his pet subjects of reminiscence', happens to live there. Such action may provoke violent thoughts within your spouse, especially if you hand them a crowbar: 'For some reason Miranda always made me think wistfully of blunt instruments.'[33] The situation can become more awkward, if later the other woman is murdered.

Surprise is one way to spice up a marriage but think carefully about the sort of surprise you are going for, as some have more repercussions than others. If you are unsure what to go for, here are some suggestions from Dagobert:

☛ Enter your spouse into a competition for a holiday without telling them first. **Surprise rating: 2/10**

☛ Take them to a fancy hotel when they've packed for a rustic hiking trip. **Surprise rating: 4/10**

☛ Acquire a four-poster Tudor bed so big you have to move into a new flat to accommodate it.
Surprise rating: 6/10

☛ Take them to Southend for the weekend and stay six months. **Surprise rating: 8/10**

☛ Buy a rare manuscript by an obscure poet, which costs exactly what you have in your joint account. **Surprise rating: 10/10**

However, bear in mind that even with surprises, there can be too much of a good thing. Dagobert's wife certainly agrees, remarking: 'I have been married to Dagobert for nearly two years, and I have never had a dull moment. I could do with a dull moment.'[34]

Think twice before using jealousy as a way of putting a spark back into your marriage. Some couples realise the foolishness of this before trying it, such as sleuthing duo Tommy and Tuppence Beresford. When Tommy asks her 'Shall I neglect you a little? … Take other women about to night clubs,' she replies:

> *'Useless … You would only meet me there with other men. And I should know perfectly well that you didn't care for the other women whereas you will never be quite sure that I didn't care for the other men.'*[35]

While the CCSRU archives show some success with making a spouse jealous,[36] it is an unpredictable strategy, as you run the risk of falling in love with the person you are pretending to show an interest in. One of Parker Pyne's plans[37] comes a cropper due to this.

Fake suicide attempts are also not recommended as a way of getting attention from your spouse. Apart from anything else, there is a possibility, especially if you are an unpleasant person, like Enid Marley, that someone may try to 'assist' you and make your pretence a reality.[38]

Long Time No See

In the main, encounters with your ex in a classic crime novel do not end well. Either they intend to kill you or use you in some way, or after meeting you they will be killed or their new partner will, leaving you thoroughly incriminated. Here are some case study-based tips our researchers compiled:

1. Patricia McGerr's *Follow as the Night*

Don't attend meals hosted by your ex, especially if they are also inviting their fiancé, their current wife and their mistress. Such a combination will make for a tense meal and puts the host in a suspicious light, as to what their real purpose is.

2. Christie's *Towards Zero*

The same applies for going on holiday with your ex. Our advice is to book yourself a separate trip, preferably in a different country!

3 and 4. Guy Cullingford's *Framed for Hanging* and Annie Haynes's *The Abbey Court Murder*

Don't meet your ex alone in their own home, nor have blazing rows with their new partner. If they die, or their partner does, you have seriously incriminated yourself.

5. Margot Bennett's *The Widow of Bath*

Don't even go back to their place for a drink with others present. This sounds like a safe situation, yet you can still find yourself entangled in murder and giving your ex an alibi. Also bear in mind that a toxic ex won't bring out the best in you and may damage new relationships.

KEY SKILL

The Death Letter

The only missive worse than a poison pen letter is the death threat. They can appear in all kinds of places, including inside Christmas crackers,[39] and not all of them are communicated in written form. Death threats can be highly creative in the classic crime universe, from pigs' heads[40] to stick figures and orange pips.[41]

Threatening letters can be sent for many reasons. One of the main motives is a perceived past wrong for which the letter writer wants revenge, examples of which have been recorded by Julian Symons in his short report 'The Santa Claus Club'[42] and Glyn Carr in his longer study, *Death Finds a Foothold*. Another common reason is the threatened person being tight with money or having recently inherited a lot of money that other people were hoping to receive themselves. Patricia Wentworth focuses on such a case in *Lonesome Road*.

However, the classic crime universe contains a variety of motives, some more unusual than others ...

Spending too much money

Further reading: Leo Bruce's 'Beef for Christmas',[43] which goes to show that not all millionaires are skinflints.

To stop someone marrying again

Further reading: John Dickson Carr's *It Walks by Night*

To stop someone opening a grave, the letter writer fearing a curse will be unleashed if it is

Further reading: Ianthe Jerrold's *Let Him Lie*

So if you ever find yourself in the unfortunate situation of receiving such a message, overleaf are our top tips for dodging your doomed fate.

Don't invite all the possible senders of the threat to a remote country house, especially if it might snow.

Sources: J. Jefferson Farjeon's *The Oval Table* and Virginia Rath's *Death at Dayton's Folly*

Don't destroy the threatening letters, as this hinders any investigation into who might have sent them.

Source: Eilís Dillon's *Death in the Quadrangle*

Don't attempt to identify and trap the would-be assassin by yourself, especially if murder attempts have already occurred.

Source: Dorothy Bowers's *Deed Without a Name*

Having made it through another day in the world of classic crime, you decide it is time for bed. After all, you have had a busy day. You stick to your usual bedtime routine tonight and head to the kitchen to wash up your cups and plates. Sponge in hand, you glance outside the window at your garden, the rain finally having stopped. The trees cast long shadows in the moonlight. However, one shadow arrests your attention; one shadow which does not look like all the rest …

How on earth did that get there? That is definitely the shadow of a man on the grass – and he isn't moving. A corpse in the garden. Typical! You knew you should have got the red gate fixed. This is hardly the time to have the police swarming over your property. It's gone 10.30. You might have death on the lawn, but you fear it might be death of the lawn, with all those heavy boots trampling all over it. Death before bedtime is so inconvenient. You will get no sleep at all if you are kept up for hours with questioning. But what should you do about the man in the moonlight?

LESSON 7
A Murder Is Announced

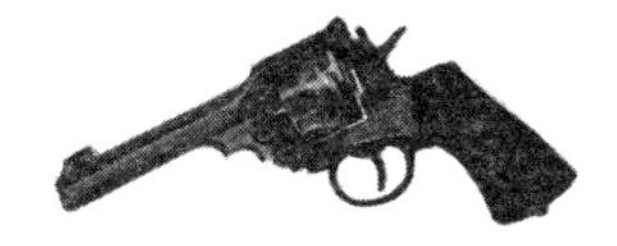

With a corpse in the garden, you have some serious decisions to make – and fast! Concealing a body is far from easy, as you know, but what if the police wrongly arrest you for the crime? It is your garden, after all …

Hide the Body!

Should you move the body? Your kneejerk reaction might be to do so, especially if it implicates you or someone else by its location. Yet this decision is fraught with risk, so much so that the CCSRU recommends leaving the body where it is and alerting the police. Nevertheless, if you are determined to relocate your corpse there are many options available. E. C. R. Lorac includes in *Bats in the Belfry* a handy list of corpse disposal methods:

- Transport the corpse in a car you bought with a deposit and bury the victim under a garage at a property you have taken in the suburbs.
- Put the corpse into a deep hole in a dene.
- Put the corpse into a sunken bath and then concrete over and place a bathmat on top.
- Place the corpse in an old coffin stored away in an old family vault.

A lack of choice is unlikely to be an issue, as you can see, but it is important to weigh up the pros and cons before committing to a particular method.

THE GOOD BODY DISPOSAL GUIDE: SIX METHODS EVALUATED

Method no. 1: Burying your corpse in a wood
Pros: Will take longer to be discovered if the wood is not frequently visited.
Cons: Potential for bad blisters, especially if you are indecisive, as repeatedly burying and digging up the body is hard work, and also fiddly if you wish to get the soil out of the victim's clothing.
Source: Jack Trevor's *The Trouble with Harry*

Method no. 2: Dumping your corpse in a river
Pros: An efficient means of distancing the corpse

from you, if you read up on currents and tides.
Cons: There is a risk of being seen by passers-by and it is hard to act nonchalant while holding a body.
Source: Pamela Branch's *The Wooden Overcoat*

Method no. 3: Stick the corpse in the deep freeze
Pros: Slows down decomposition, which buys you time while you find a better place to put it.
Cons: You will have to find somewhere else to store your ice cream and there is always the outside chance of a third party scuppering your plans if they realise the body is there.
Source: Richard Shattuck's *The Wedding Guest Sat on a Stone*

Method no. 4: Dumping the body on to someone else's property
Pros: You get the bonus of getting revenge on someone you don't like.
Cons: It is very hard to get rid of the trail leading back to yourself.
Sources: Agatha Christie's *The Body in the Library,* John Donavan's *Case of the Talking Dust* and Dorothy L. Sayers's *Whose Body?*

Method no. 5: Bury the corpse in a cellar
Pros: Unlikely to be discovered for a long time if covered with cement.
Cons: Discovery is likely if you only cover the body with soil. Loose earth inevitably encourages digging, especially if a new homeowner is an imaginative sort who expects to find buried treasure.
Source: Anthony Berkeley's *Murder in the Basement*

Method no. 6: Burn the body along with a kangaroo's corpse. Sift any metal from the ashes and dissolve with acid. Crush any bones into dust.

Pros: An incredibly thorough method which makes identification hard.

Cons: It is messy, requires a lot of peace and quiet to complete unobserved, and unless you live in Australia you will find it difficult to obtain a kangaroo.

Source: Arthur *Upfield's The Sands of Windee*[1]

KEY SKILL

A Little Gentle Sleuthing

One of the most popular hobbies in the classic crime universe is amateur sleuthing. But what do you need to know before trying it? Here are our top tips …

- ☛ Start a hobby which gives you a legitimate excuse to be outside. Participating in this hobby will provide good camouflage for your real purpose of observing others. Miss Marple recommends gardening and birdwatching, especially the latter, which gives you the perfect defence for using your binoculars.[2]

- ☛ If your snooping takes you into other people's properties, prepare an excuse beforehand for being there in case you get caught. One man who did not was Ty Grant, who sums up the problems of what to do when you have been caught reading a suspect's love letters by torchlight: 'A casual remark seems out of place, no apology is adequate and you are in no position to start anything on your own account.'[3]

- ☛ If trailing a suspect is not your forte, delegate this task to someone else less conspicuous. You can't be great at everything, as Dr Fell concludes: 'If I were to attempt shadowing anybody, the shadowee would find himself about as inconspicuous as though he were to walk down Piccadilly pursued by the Albert Memorial.'[4] However, as Miss Marple points out, if you are an older woman your sleuthing activities will naturally be less noticeable.[5]

- ☛ Before beginning any snooping, think carefully about what you will and won't do to forward the case. Often snooping disturbs the privacy of others, which some find uncomfortable, as Ellery Queen attests: 'Now, while eavesdropping is an affront to hospitality, it is an essential to the business of detection; and the great question in

Ellery's mind was: Was he first a guest, or was he first a detective?'[6]

- ☛ Be prepared for some hostility or at least a lukewarm attitude from the police investigating the case. Your help initially may not be appreciated, but once you've found the crook this will hopefully change.

- ☛ Finally, bear in mind that snooping can make you unpopular if you practise it outside murder cases. Feathers may be ruffled in your local area, and you could encourage murderous thoughts towards yourself. If Ethel Tither had dialled back her curiosity, she might have been spared an ignominious fate inside a cesspool.[7]

The Scene of the Crime

When you first find a body, it is hard to stay calm. Your mind is in a whirl, with multiple thoughts and feelings jostling for attention. With the stress mounting, it can be all too easy to make mistakes: mistakes which put you straight to the top of the police suspect list. So to help you stay cool under the pressure, here is our simple AH HA method:

☛ Alert the Authorities

As much as you might want to, you can't look the other way and pretend the body is not there. Calling the police in may spoil the mood of your social gathering and police suspicion will rest upon you if you raise the alarm first, but it is far more awkward to be asked later to explain why you saw the body and didn't do anything.[8]

☛ Handkerchief Hands

We all know touching anything at a crime scene is a bad idea, given the potential for incriminating ourselves and angering the police, but sometimes it seems unavoidable …

'Of course I haven't touched anything! … Well, how could I telephone you without handling the telephone? … Yes, it's here in the room… Well, how sharper than a serpent's tooth is an ungrateful – what's that? … Come to think of it, I needn't have called you at all. Next time I'll let you find your own body…'[9]

To dodge such a conversation yourself, we recommend carefully using a handkerchief to touch any necessary items.

☛ HANDS IN POCKETS

Seriously, DO NOT TOUCH ANYTHING! Especially the object which killed the corpse. It might be an unconscious action of picking up a fallen object,[10] or you may be struggling with curiosity or have an ungovernable need to be tidy, but whatever the motivation, touching the weapon spells disaster. This might constitute a tough grilling from the police, a full-blown murder trial or even time on the run.[11]

☛ ABSTRACT NOTHING

A crime scene is not a souvenir shop, full of mementos to take home and remember it by. Nor is it your job to play God and decide which criminals escape punishment. Muddying the investigative waters by tampering with the scene can have fatal consequences, enabling further murders to be committed. How do you know you won't be one of them? After all, are you sure you know who did the crime?[12]

Don't Lie to the Police

We all know that withholding evidence from the police is not a good idea, primarily because it increases our chances of being killed, or increases that risk for others in our family or social group. The CCSRU archives are full of case studies that prove this point, from Maureen Sarsfield's *Murder at Beechlands* to Dorothy Cole Meade's *Death Over Her Shoulder*. We say we would never act so foolishly, but there are many reasons for withholding information from the police. Which reason below would most persuade you to break the golden rule?

- ❑ Your mother told you to.
  Source: Margaret Ann Hubbard's *Murder Takes the Veil*

- ❑ To make your own amateur sleuth investigation look better.
  Source: John Rowland's *Calamity in Kent*

- ❑ To shield a stranger you are attracted to.
  Source: J. Jefferson Farjeon's *The Z Murders*

- ❑ You live in a community which dislikes telling on one another. Live and let live is your motto.
  Source: E. C. R. Lorac's *Murder in the Mill Race*

- ❑ To commit blackmail.
  Source: Christie's *The Mirror Crack'd from Side to Side*

- ❑ You strongly dislike the victim.
  Source: Anthony Berkeley's *Jumping Jenny*

- ❑ You want to preserve the memory of the victim.
  Source: E. C. R. Lorac's *Post after Post-Mortem*

- ❑ You want to shield someone close to you, who is implicated in the crime.
  Source: John Dickson Carr's *The Seat of the Scornful*

KEY SKILL

Step in the Dark

Keen to do some night-time sleuthing? Then keep these tips in mind:

- Hold on to your torch. Don't let anyone else get a hold of it and don't drop it. Maybe bring a spare one if you know you have butterfingers.[13]

- Never investigate suspicious night-time activities alone in case an intruder turns violent. This is especially important if the location is a sinister, seemingly empty house (it isn't).[14]

- On no account conduct any night-time investigation if one or more of the following applies:

  – There's a storm raging outside.[15]

  – There is a power cut.[16]

  – There is a serial killer on the loose.[17]

  – You are wearing pyjamas. This is especially applicable if it is snowing.[18]

Wanted for Questioning

Being questioned by the police is inevitable if you are in the vicinity of a crime. If you have adhered to the earlier advice on how to deal with a crime scene you will hopefully have gained some police approval. However, you are not out of the woods yet. One wrong word and you could incorrectly be deemed a prime suspect. Here are some mistakes you should avoid:

Case study: *Murder on the Blackboard*
Author: Stuart Palmer
Date: 1932
Suspect: Hildegarde Withers
What the suspect did: Used biting sarcasm
What the suspect should have done: While she avoided jail, Miss Withers isolated herself from the police investigation and therefore any information they might have that she did not. Holding back the insults is a wise move if you want to be on harmonious terms with the police.

Case study: *The Seat of the Scornful*
Author: John Dickson Carr
Date: 1942
Suspect: Mr Justice Ireton
What the suspect did: Despite being incriminated by circumstantial evidence, he dismantles all police theories which would absolve him. The icing on the cake is his reticence in response

to all police questions.

What the suspect should have done: Let the police explore their alternative theories, as even a wrong theory might unearth some new facts.

Case study: *Death on the Nile*
Author: Agatha Christie
Date: 1937
Suspect: Louise Bourget
What the suspect did: Loudly announced she had some important information for the police and then delayed passing it on to the appropriate authorities.
What the suspect should have done: Immediately told the police what she knew. Ignoring this rule inevitably led to her demise shortly afterwards.

Case study: *Under the Influence*
Author: Geoffrey Kerr
Date: 1953
Suspect: Harry Browne
What the suspect did: Warned the police of a forthcoming murder and when questioned how he knew about it, stated he read the murderer's mind (a talent he can only manage while drunk).
What the suspect should have done: Whether it is true or not, alcohol-induced mind reading is unlikely to convince the police. Gathering more

concrete facts about the killing first would have given his story more credence.

On the Run

Perhaps your police interview went badly, or you have cracked under the pressure of circumstantial evidence. Deciding to go on the run is a big step to take. If you have plenty of cash you will have more options, such as buying false passports, but money isn't everything when it comes to the perfect escape from the law.[19]

Having appropriate equipment is important. Knowing what to take is largely common sense: pyjamas, toothpaste, toiletries, emergency food rations, but …

WATSON'S WONDERFUL COMBINATION WATCH-DOG AND WATER-PISTOL

This handy device has two main functions:

1. To frighten away aggressors.
2. To alert passers-by that you need help.

BUT WAIT: IT DOES MORE THAN THAT!

Picture the scene ...

Only 5s 6d!

EPILOGUE
The Perfect Murder

Ahh. At last. Peace and quiet. You can finally enjoy your cup of cocoa, unlike last night. Such a relief the police have finally left. Even they were surprised by how quickly they solved the case of the body on the lawn. The killer should never have worn an old woollen jumper under their coat. It was incredibly bad luck that a loose thread caught on the victim and even more unfortunate that the thread did not break. Instead, the jumper unravelled with each step the killer took, leaving the most painfully embarrassing trail for the police to follow. If only you could have been there when the culprit was apprehended. Their shocked and surprised face, only then seeing the tangled skein at their feet, which used to be their favourite jumper. That is a grave mistake to learn from, for when you – I mean, if *you – ever need to kill again. Yes, again, as today has been quite a busy day for you – getting away with murder.*

The memories of the last twenty-four hours begin to flood back. It all began the previous evening when there was a knock. There was somebody at the door. Your unexpected caller was an old school friend – well, 'friend' is pushing it, since they spent most of their time tormenting you. You thought it was bad enough when this intruder had the temerity to ask for a bed for the night, before they went on holiday the next day, but worse was to follow. It stuck in your throat when they suggested how much nicer it was to stay with an old chum than put up at a hotel. They were always keen to avoid spending their own money, despite having plenty of it. They had expected no disagreement with this plan, so much so that they had sent a postcard to Carter Paterson beforehand to collect their holiday trunk from your address. The cheek!

Once your friend had taken the best chair in the living room, the snide remarks soon began to fall. You mentally braced yourself for an uncomfortable hour or two before bed, but the barbed comments took an unexpected turn. More than one hinted at that unfortunate episode during sixth form. A simple misunderstanding! Yet it soon transpired that your 'friend' had a different opinion. Far from keeping it quiet, they felt a strong conviction to send your employer a well-timed letter. Unless of course you could convince them otherwise. You began to see why your 'friend' always had so much money …

Such a letter would scupper your chances of promotion. Your 'friend' thought they had you checkmate, but it was only checkmate to murder. It was time for a necessary end – to their life. You smiled to yourself. For all their cunning your 'friend' had not followed many rules of survival in the classic crime universe. Don't you remember that no blackmailer should expect free accommodation from their victims?

Their mistakes continued when they accepted your offer of a bedtime dark hot chocolate, compounded by them failing to watch you in the kitchen as you made it. In the fatal five minutes, it was easy to lace their drink with potassium cyanide. You had been using it to deal with some pesky wasps that wouldn't leave. Not much has changed, you quip to yourself.

They say murder isn't easy and that crime pays no dividends. You beg to differ. Then again, your 'friend' did helpfully provide you with a ready-made coffin with their holiday trunk. You tucked them inside before rigor mortis had set in and it was not too laborious a task to burn their identifying papers. As to the rest of their belongings, you thought it was right that charity started at home and packaged up their clothes. You are sure St Dunstan's appreciated their donation. You certainly appreciated yours from their wallet. Nice of your 'friend' to finally do you a good turn.

The clean-up in the morning went without a hitch, except nearly forgetting to take the trunk out with the rest of the rubbish. Nevertheless, you were on time for the collection from Carter Paterson – so kind of your 'friend' to organise that for you! It was beginner's luck that the weather was foggy. It made it so much easier for you to make your fall over the trunk look like an accident. The sore shins were worth it, for that fall gave you the chance to exchange the sender's address details. After all, you hardly wanted the hotel in Marrakesh to trace the unfortunate trunk contents back to your door.

Remembering all this, your thoughts turn to your future, a vista of possibilities on the horizon. You stretch out in front of the fire and raise your mug to having a wonderful crime.

ACKNOWLEDGEMENTS

I hope you have enjoyed reading this book, and that if you ever find yourself stuck in a classic crime novel you will be able to avoid the many pitfalls. This 'guide' is based on many years' worth of reading, but not just my own. Classic crime fiction is so wonderfully varied, with thousands upon thousands of titles, that it would have been a very different book if I had been confined to my own reading: I would have missed many peculiar and varied examples. So I would like to thank the following people, who I consider to be my online classic crime fiction-championing compatriots: Steven Barge, Aidan Brack, Martin Edwards, Curtis Evans, Brad Friedman, Bev Hankins, John Harrison, John Norris, Jim Noy, Carol McBride, Rekha Rao and Moira Redmond. Whether it was a blog post pointing me in the direction of a useful book or patient answering of my many seemingly bizarre and pedantic questions, your help was much appreciated.

NOTES

Lesson 1

1. Dickson, C. (1934). *The White Priory Murders*. London: British Library, 2022, p. 200.
2. In the text and notes of this book, Agatha Christie is often mentioned by surname only, for the sake of brevity.
3. Brown, F. (1950). *Night of the Jabberwock*. Eugene, OR: Bruin Books, 2017, p. 22.
4. Gilbert, A. (1971). *Tenant for the Tomb*. New York: Ballantine Books, p. 57.
5. See Agatha Christie's *A Murder is Announced* (1950).
6. See Christie's 'Wireless' (1926), 'The Face of Helen' (1927) and Ngaio Marsh's 'Death on the Air' (1937). Marsh's story is included in *A Surprise for Christmas* (2020), ed. by Martin Edwards.
7. See E. C. R. Lorac's *These Names Make Clues* (1937) and John Bude's *Death Knows No Calendar* (1942).
8. Rice, L. (1938). *Well Dressed for Murder*. Greenville, OH: Coachwhip Publications, 2019, p. 91.
9. See Christie's *Three Act Tragedy* (1934).
10. See Delano Ames's *Crime Out of Mind* (1956).
11. See Ruth Rendell's *A Judgement in Stone* (1977).
12. Macdonald, P. (1924). *The Rasp*. London: Collins Crime Club, 2015, p. 21.
13. See John Dickson Carr's *The Hollow Man* (1935) and Anthony Berkeley's *The Layton Court Mystery* (1925).

14. See Christie's 'Motive v Opportunity' (1928).
15. Sayers, D. L. (2017). Review of *Murder Is Easy* (1933) by Armstrong Livingston. In Edwards, M. (ed.), *Taking Detective Fiction Seriously: The Collected Crime Reviews of Dorothy L. Sayers*. Perth: Tippermuir, p. 77.
16. Cox, A. B. (1925). *Jugged Journalism*. London: Herbert Jenkins, p. 35.
17. See Charles J. Dutton's *Murder at the Library* (1931).
18. See Victor L. Whitechurch's *Crime at Diana's Pool* (1926) and Patricia Wentworth's *The Silent Pool* (1954).
19. See Frances and Richard Lockridge's *With One Stone* (1961) and Dana Chambers's *The Case of Caroline Animus* (1946).
20. See G. K. Chesterton's 'The Vengeance of the Statue' (1922).
21. See Cyril Hare's *An English Murder* (1951).
22. See Margot Bennett's *Time to Change Hats* (1945).
23. See Earl Derr Biggers's *The Chinese Parrot* (1926) and Anne Austin's *The Avenging Parrot* (1930).
24. The Sherlock Holmes story is 'The Blue Carbuncle' (1892), which can be found in *Silent Nights* (2015), ed. by Martin Edwards. A thief unwisely conceals a stolen jewel inside a goose, in the run-up to Christmas. What could possibly go wrong?

Lesson 2

1. This story can be found in *Policeman's Lot* (1933).
2. This story is included in *Blood on the Tracks* (2018), ed. by Martin Edwards.
3. This story is included in *Capital Crimes* (2015), ed. by Martin Edwards.
4. See Sébastien Japrisot's *The Sleeping Car Murders* (1962).
5. Her tribulations can be read in Lorna Nicholl Morgan's *Another Little Christmas Murder* (1947).
6. Such a set-up features in Molly Thynne's *The Crime at Noah's Ark* (1931).
7. See J. Jefferson Farjeon's *Mystery in White* (1938).
8. Gilbert, A (1945). *Don't Open the Door!*. London: Collins Crime Club, 1949, p. 95.

9. This story is included in Charlotte Armstrong's *Night Call and Other Stories* (2014).
10. See Louisa Revell's *The Bus Station Murders* (1947). Even if you avoid being the victim, you will still have the trial of being under suspicion for the crime.
11. See Leslie Cargill's *Death Goes by Bus* (1936).
12. See Patrick Leyton's *The Crime with Ten Solutions* (1935) and Ethel Lina White's *The Third Eye* (1937).
13. John Rhode's book echoes another true crime case, the murder of Julia Wallace in 1931.
14. This example proves that such hoaxes can even happen to the police, who in this instance leave their station due to a hoax call, only to return and find their colleague dead.
15. Some examples include: Helen McCloy's *He Never Came Back* (1954), Rae Foley's *Dangerous to Me* (1959) and John Le Carré's *Smiley's People* (1979).
16. See: *Grey Mask* (1928), *The Case of William Smith* (1948), *Ladies' Bane* (1952) and *The Listening Eye* (1955).
17. This story is included in *Deep Waters* (2019), ed. by Martin Edwards.
18. See Ursula Curtiss's *The Deadly Climate* (1955).
19. See Margery Allingham's 'On Christmas Day in the Morning' (1950), which is included in *A Surprise for Christmas* (2020), ed. by Martin Edwards.
20. Lorac, E. C. R. (1952). *Murder in the Mill Race*. London: British Library, 2019, p. 37.
21. See John Franklin Bardin's *The Last of Philip Banter* (1947) and Robert Hare's *The Doctor's First Murder* (1933).
22. See Henrietta Clandon's *Good by Stealth* (1936).

Lesson 3

1. These criteria were compiled from various sources housed at the CCSRU, including: E. C. Bentley's *Trent's Last Case* (1913), Arthur Conan Doyle's *The Valley of Fear* (1914), Agatha Christie's *The Murder of Roger Ackroyd* (1926), Margery

Allingham's *Flowers for the Judge* (1936), C. H. B. Kitchin's *Death of His Uncle* (1939) and Erle Stanley Gardner's *The Case of the Smoking Chimney* (1942).

2. See Freeman Wills Crofts's *The Box Office Murders* (1929).
3. Tuppence and Tommy Beresford wrote this advert in Christie's *The Secret Adversary* (1922). While ultimately things turn out well for them, initially Tuppence is assumed to be a blackmailer.
4. See Christie's *They Came to Baghdad* (1951).
5. Patricia Wentworth's *Fool Errant* (1929) and John Russell Fearn's *The Rattenbury Mystery* (1955) include examples of this.
6. See Nicholas Blake's *There's Trouble Brewing* (1937), Margaret Armstrong's *Murder in Stained Glass* (1939) and Ruth Sawtell Wallis's *Too Many Bones* (1943), respectively.
7. See June Wright's *Murder in the Telephone Exchange* (1948) and Cyril Hare's *With a Bare Bodkin* (1946).
8. See Lucille Fletcher's *Eighty Dollars to Stamford* (1975).
9. See Doyle's 'The Adventure of the Copper Beeches' (1892), which is included in *Murder at the Manor* (2016), ed. by Martin Edwards. In this story Violet Hunter is offered a salary of £120 p.a. as a governess, if she cuts her hair short.
10. See Arthur Conan Doyle's 'The Red-headed League' (1891).
11. White, E. L. (1942). 'Cheese'. In: Edwards, M. (ed.), *Capital Crimes*. London: British Library, 2015, pp. 279–96 (p. 281).
12. See J. J. Connington's *The Sweepstake Murders* (1931). Other examples appear in: Ellery Queen's 'The Gettysburg Bugle' (1951) in *Calendar of Crime* (1952), Edwin Balmer and Philip Wylie's *Five Fatal Words* (1932) and Will Levinrew's *Death Points a Finger* (1933).
13. See Helen McCloy's *The Deadly Truth* (1943).
14. See Christie's *Black Coffee* (1930) and Patricia Wentworth's *The Key* (1944), respectively.
15. Dillon, E. (1956). *Death in the Quadrangle*. Lyons, CO: Rue Morgue Press, 2010, p. 24.

16. See Joan Fleming's *Miss Bones* (1959).
17. Victoria Jones falls foul of this problem in Christie's *They Came to Baghdad* (1951).
18. Tilton, A. (1937). *Beginning with a Bash*. Rockville, MD: Wildside Press, 2018, p. 57.
19. See Bruce Graeme's *A Case of Books* (1946), Bernard J. Farmer's *Death of a Bookseller* (1956), Carolyn Wells's *Murder in the Bookshop* (1936) and Augusto De Angelis's *Death in a Bookstore* (1936).
20. See Agnes Miller's *The Colfax Book-Plate* (1926) for an unusual example of this type of mystery, where the central murder revolves around a book with a rare book plate inside.
21. Witting, C. (1937). *Murder in Blue*. Plymouth: Galileo, 2021, p. 41.
22. Campbell, R. T. (1946). *Bodies in a Bookshop*. New York: Dover, 1984, p. 22.
23. See Vernon Loder's *The Shop Window Murders* (1930).
24. Witting, C. (1937). *Midsummer Murder*. London: Hodder & Stoughton, 1953, p. 12.
25. See Anthony Gilbert's 'Give Me a Ring' (1955), which is included in *A Surprise for Christmas* (2020), ed. by Martin Edwards.
26. See Ngaio Marsh's *Light Thickens* (1982), Marvin Kaye's *Bullets for Macbeth* (1976) and Lange Lewis's *Juliet Dies Twice* (1943), respectively.
27. See Ngaio Marsh's *Overture to Death* (1939).
28. See Ngaio Marsh's *Opening Night* (1951).
29. See Cyril Hare's *When the Wind Blows* (1949).
30. See Christie's *They Do It with Mirrors* (1952) and Ngaio Marsh's *Vintage Murder* (1937).
31. Examples feature in Ngaio Marsh's *Death at the Dolphin* (1967) and Clifford Witting's *Measure for Murder* (1941).
32. See Caryl Brahms and S. J. Simon's *Casino for Sale* (1938).

Lesson 4

1. The British Newspaper Archive notes the 'moral panic of the 1920s and 1930s' surrounding dance halls, with a particular anxiety around female intoxication. For further information see: https://blog.britishnewspaperarchive.co.uk/2019/10/15/a-look-at-the-history-of-dance-halls.
2. Examples occur in Ellery Queen's *The Roman Hat Mystery* (1929), Elizabeth Gill's *What Dread Hand* (1932) and John Dickson Carr's *Panic in Box C* (1966).
3. See Agatha Christie's *The ABC Murders* (1936).
4. Carr, John Dickson (1931). *Castle Skull*. London: British Library, 2020, p. 20.
5. See Helen McCloy's *Dance of Death* (1938).
6. See June Wright's *Reservation for Murder* (1958).
7. See Brian Flynn's *The Creeping Jenny* (1933).
8. See Kelley Roos's *Necessary Evil* (1965).
9. See Doris Miles Disney's *Straw Man* (1951).
10. Another example of a murderous game of hide and seek can be found in Edmund Crispin's 'The Hours of Darkness' (1949), which is included in *Bodies from the Library 2* (2019), ed. by Tony Medawar. Hide and seek can also provide criminal conspirators with long periods of time to confer with each other, without being overheard, as evidenced in Mary Kelly's *Due to a Death* (1962).
11. This story is included in Ellery Queen's *Calendar of Crime* (1952).
12. Other examples of delivering ultimatums or bad news at dinner appear in Michael Innes's *There Came Both Mist and Snow* (1940) and Mavis Doriel Hay's *The Santa Klaus Murder* (1936).
13. Another example is recorded in Catherine Aird's *Slight Mourning* (1975).
14. Examples include John Dickson Carr's *The Sleeping Sphinx* (1947), in which the party's theme is the masks of executed murderers, and Gladys Mitchell's *Watson's Choice* (1955), in which guests are asked to come as characters from the Sherlock Holmes stories.

15. See Christie's 'The Affair at the Victory Ball' (1923) and 'Finessing the King' (1924).
16. Christie chronicles this case in 'The Idol House of Astarte' (1928), which is included in *The Thirteen Problems* (1932).
17. This story is included in *The Christmas Card Crime and Other Stories* (2018), ed. by Martin Edwards.
18. See Ngaio Marsh's *Death in a White Tie* (1938).
19. Witting, C. (1939). *Catt Out of the Bag*. London: Hodder & Stoughton, 1952, pp. 108–9.
20. Witting, C. (1939). *Catt Out of the Bag*. London: Hodder & Stoughton, 1952, p. 122.
21. An example of this features in Ellery Queen's *The Finishing Stroke* (1958).
22. See Fredric Brown's *Murder Can Be Fun* (1948).
23. This story is included in *Silent Nights: Christmas Mysteries* (2015), ed. by Martin Edwards.
24. See Christie's *Why Didn't They Ask Evans?* (1934).
25. See A. G. Macdonell's *The Factory on the Cliff* (1928).
26. This story is included in *Settling Scores* (2020), ed. by Martin Edwards.
27. See Christie's *Cat Among the Pigeons* (1959).
28. See Bernard Newman's 'Death at the Wicket' (1956), which is included in *Settling Scores* (2020), ed. by Martin Edwards.

Lesson 5

1. The first Butlin's holiday camp opened in 1937 and the first Youth Hostel Association accommodation in 1930. The 1930s saw a huge increase in holidaymaking, partially due to more UK employers giving paid holidays to their staff. The 1938 Holidays Pay Act was another factor.
2. See Alice Campbell's *Spider Web* (1938).
3. See Arthur Conan Doyle's *The Hound of the Baskervilles* (1902), Thomas Kindon's *Murder in the Moor* (1929) and Agatha Christie's *The Sittaford Mystery* (1931).

4. See Ethel Lina White's *The Lady Vanishes* (1936).
5. See Josephine Tey's *A Shilling for Candles* (1936).
6. Ames, D. (1953). *No Mourning for the Matador*. London: Hodder & Stoughton, p. 19.
7. See Patricia Wentworth's *The Dower House* (1925).
8. High stress levels when trying to make this decision have been reported in case studies such as Celia Fremlin's *Uncle Paul* (1959).
9. Sayers, D. L. (1932). *Have His Carcase*. London: Harper Collins, 2012, p. 3.
10. See Delano Ames's *Corpse Diplomatique* (1950).
11. Brand, C. (1955). *Tour de Force*. London: Penguin, 1957, p. 8.
12. This story is included in *Continental Crimes* (2017), ed. by Martin Edwards.
13. Christie, A. (1924). *The Man in the Brown Suit*. London: Harper Collins, 2017, p. 118.
14. Ames, D. (1952). *Murder, Maestro, Please*. New York: Perennial Library, 1983, p. 8.
15. Ames, D. (1952). *Murder, Maestro, Please*. New York: Perennial Library, 1983, p. 9.
16. See Charlotte Armstrong's 'Protector of Travellers' (1965), which is included in *Night Call and Other Stories of Suspense* (2014).
17. Brand, C. (1955). *Tour de Force*. London: Penguin, 1957, p. 11.
18. Ames, D. (1950). *Corpse Diplomatique*. New York: Perennial Library, 1983, p. 70.
19. See John and Emery Bonett's *No Grave for a Lady* (1959).
20. Melville, A. (1936). *Death of Anton*. London: British Library, 2015, p. 26.
21. See Vincent Starrett's *The Great Hotel Murder* (1935).
22. See Nicholas Blake's *Malice in Wonderland* (1940).
23. See Christie's *Appointment with Death* (1938).
24. See M. M. Kaye's *Death in Cyprus* (1956).
25. See C. A. Alington's 'The Adventure of the Dorset Squire' (1937), which is included in *Bodies from the Library 2* (2019), ed. by Tony Medawar.

26. Brand, C. (1955). *Tour de Force*. London: Penguin, 1957, p. 35.
27. Christie, A. (1930). *The Murder at the Vicarage*. London: HarperCollins, 2016, p. 18.
28. See Eric Ambler's *Passage of Arms* (1959), which sees someone thinking it would be a good idea to help aid a dubious arms sale while on holiday.

Lesson 6

1. Gilbert, A. (1961). *She Shall Die*. Bath: Chivers Press, 2003, p. 8.
2. Christie, A. (1951). *They Came to Baghdad*. London: HarperCollins, 2017, p. 17.
3. See Julian Symons's *The Colour of Murder* (1957).
4. See Anthony Gilbert's *Death in Fancy Dress* (1933).
5. See D. B. Olsen's *Gallows for the Groom* (1947).
6. Lombard, N. (1943). *Murder's a Swine*. London: British Library, 2021, p. 44.
7. See Ethel Lina White's *Step in the Dark* (1938).
8. This unusual tip comes from James Norman's *Murder, Chop, Chop* (1942).
9. Brand, C. (1952). *Fog of Doubt*. New York: Mysterious Press, 2013, p. 117.
10. See Brian Flynn's *The Mystery of the Peacock's Eye* (1928), where Anthony Bathurst flirts with a woman using algebra.
11. Offord, L. (1941). *The Nine Dark Hours*. New York: Felony & Mayhem, 2018, p. 60.
12. See Arthur Conan Doyle's 'The Adventure of Charles Augustus Milverton' (1904) and Annie Haynes's *The House in Charlton Crescent* (1926) and *The Crime at Tattenham Corner* (1927).
13. See John Bude's *Death in White Pyjamas* (1944).
14. See Christopher St John Sprigg's *Crime in Kensington* (1933).
15. Macdonell, A. (1928). *The Factory on the Cliff*. Stroud: Fonthill Media, 2021, p. 32.
16. Brand, C. (1948). *Death of Jezebel*. London: British Library, 2022, p. 129.

17. See Charlotte Armstrong's *Mischief* (1950).
18. See Patricia Wentworth's *The Brading Collection* (1950).
19. See June Wright's *Reservation for Murder* (1958). The most exciting conversation Mary Allen can look forward to with her accountant beau, Cyril, is on the state of each other's health and his views on legal policies.
20. Ibid.
21. Ibid.
22. See Doris Miles Disney's *Do Not Fold, Spindle or Mutilate* (1970).
23. Melville, A (1934). *Weekend at Thrackley*. London: British Library, 2018, p. 233.
24. Bude, J. (1952). *Death on the Riviera*. London: British Library, 2016, pp. 222–3.
25. Carr, J. (1944). *Till Death Do Us Part*. London: British Library, 2021, p. 32.
26. See Alice and Claude Askew's 'The Mystery of Chenholt' (1908) in *The Long Arm of the Law* (2017), ed. by Martin Edwards.
27. See Margery Allingham's *The Fashion in Shrouds* (1938).
28. Wright, J. (1958). *Reservation for Murder*. Portland, OR: Verse Chorus Press, 2020, p. 155.
29. Christie, A. (1971). *Nemesis*. London: HarperCollins, 2016, p. 37.
30. Doyle, A. C. (1902). *The Hound of the Baskervilles*. London: Pan Macmillan, 2016, p. 10.
31. Crane, F. (1969). *The Turquoise Shop*. Boulder, CO: Rue Morgue Press, 2004, p. 31.
32. Symons, J. (1957). *The Colour of Murder*. Scottsdale, AZ: Poisoned Pen Press, 2018, p. 59.
33. Ames, D. (1949). *Murder Begins at Home*. Boulder, CO: Rue Morgue Press, 2009, p. 14.
34. Ames, D. (1950). *Death of a Fellow Traveller*. London: Hodder & Stoughton, 1953, p. 18.
35. Christie, A. (1929). 'A Fairy in the Flat'. In: Christie, A. *Partners in Crime*. London: HarperCollins, 2015, pp. 1–9 (p. 2).

36. See Christie's 'The Case of the Middle-Aged Wife' (1932), which is included in *Parker Pyne Investigates* (1934).
37. See Christie's 'The Case of the Discontented Husband' (1932), which is included in *Parker Pyne Investigates* (1934).
38. See Pamela Branch's *Murder's Little Sister* (1958).
39. See Brian Flynn's *The Murders Near Mapleton* (1929).
40. See Nap Lombard's *Murder's a Swine* (1943).
41. See Arthur Conan Doyle's 'The Adventure of the Dancing Man' (1903) and 'The Adventure of the Five Orange Pips' (1891) respectively.
42. This story is included in *Crimson Snow: Winter Mysteries* (2016), ed. by Martin Edwards.
43. This short story is included in *Silent Nights: Christmas Mysteries* (2015), ed. by Martin Edwards.

Lesson 7

1. Upfield discussed this 'perfect' murder method with friends, one of whom decided to put it into practice. They murdered three men before being caught, and Upfield had to testify at their trial.
2. See Agatha Christie's *The Murder at the Vicarage* (1930).
3. Shattuck, R. (1940). *The Wedding Guest Sat on a Stone*. New York: Crowell-Collier, 1963, p. 52.
4. Carr, J. (1939). *The Problem of the Wire Cage*. New York: Kensington, 1986, p. 129.
5. See Christie's *A Murder is Announced* (1950).
6. Queen, E. (1935). *The Spanish Cape Mystery*. London: Gollancz, 1949, p. 174.
7. See George Bellairs' *Death of Busybody* (1942).
8. See Michael Venning's *The Man Who Slept All Day* (1942).
9. Dillon, E. (1953). *Death at Crane's Court*. New York: Harper & Row, 1988, p. 61.
10. See Patricia Wentworth's *The Fingerprint* (1959).
11. See A. A. Milne's *Four Days Wonder* (1933).
12. See Virginia Perdue's *The Singing Clock* (1941), Norman Berrow's

The Bishop's Sword and Ione Montgomery's *The Golden Dress* (1940).

13. See Ianthe Jerrold's *There May Be Danger* (1948).
14. See Christie's *Cat among the Pigeons* (1959) and Mabel Seeley's *The Listening House* (1938).
15. See Mary Roberts Rinehart's *The Bat* (1926).
16. Ibid.
17. See Ethel Lina White's *Some Must Watch* (1933).
18. See Craig Rice's *Eight Faces at Three* (1939), Molly Thynne's *The Crime at Noah's Ark* (1931) and Victor Bridges's *It Happened in Essex* (1938).
19. See Patricia Highsmith's *The Two Faces of January* (1964), in which plentiful funds do not prevent the fugitives turning on one another.